EDNY AREM

EDNY AREM

ASHOK VARMA

PARTRIDGE

A Penguin Random House Company

To order additional copies of this book, contact
Partridge India
000 800 10062 62
orders.india@partridgepublishing.com

www.partridgepublishing.com/india

To the entire team of the popular
Hindi movie of the eighties

Mr. India

1

The frenzy of the morning had subsided. Day was not so bright but the sun shone with a little bit of haziness as is usual around this time of the year in Delhi. It was neither cloudy nor really foggy but the sky still appeared more whitish than blue, thanks to the ever present smog over the city.

Nevertheless, sitting out in the weak sun with tea or pea nuts or sometimes even with some fruits was a favourite pastime of the Delhiites, particularly on holidays. But it was not a holiday for Ram Singh. He was on duty and that too on a red alert day. January 26th is always a red alert day when each nerve of every cop of the entire police force in the capital is tense, suspicious of every small unidentified object, any movement even slightly deviating from the usual, every individual on the street, slowing down of the vehicles or sudden acceleration. Instructions' galore precedes this most widely celebrated national festival of India.

But now the festivities were over. The main Republic Day function was over. The planes had flown past at low altitude showering flowers on the VVIPs seated in their special enclosure at the India Gate. Ram Singh was only few hundred metres from the heart of these activities with the skeletal staff left to man the police station and could only see the planes suddenly leaping vertically up after their flypast and then hundreds of balloons, green white and saffron, depicting the three colours of the national tricolor, swaying, slowly rising up in the air. This marked the end of the day's public ceremonies.

The policemen on special duties at the venue of the Republic day parade had also returned and were relaxing now, the climax having been over. But the red alert continued. It was to continue for the whole day and then for a couple of more days… just in case….!

The streets would wear a deserted look for the rest of the day, picking up to some extent in the evening hours. Strong traffic curbs in the morning hours and the fear of terrorist activities kept Delhiites indoors on this day. Public transport was reduced to a trickle and this was one of the very few occasions when the entire families sat glued to their television sets for most part of the morning. After the telecast of Republic Day was over, the lady would start preparing for the holiday special lunch and the fight for their favourite channels would begin amongst the children with the strongest one finally taking control of the remote!

Akbar Road police station was an easy posting. It was a VVIP area and the duties were mainly confined to traffic bandobust in front of the spacious bungalows of Ministers and MPs. Sometimes snakes entering into houses broke the monotony of their rhythmic duties. The police staff had to always be on the alert but petty criminals never dared to visit these areas and so this station was devoid of the rustle-bustle generally seen at most other police stations of the capital.

There was also no side income, except occasional bakhshish from the followers of the VVIPs. The police station had a fairly large but poorly maintained compound. It reminded Ram Singh of the open space in front of his grandfather's cottage in his village near Panipat and the long winter afternoons the whole family spent on charpoys with endless supplies of fresh foods from the farms. Here at the police station they had to be content with tea or peanuts only. That too had to be bought. With hard cash.

The mild warmth of the weak sun, the special *makke di roti* and *sarson da saag* meal sent by the mother of one of their colleagues for this special day, which they had only an hour ago and the quiet stillness of the surroundings weighed heavily on the tired eyelids of Ram Singh and he was fighting hard to stay not only awake but also alert. Slightly away from the police station, on the other side of the wide street a DTC bus stopped and a man with blue jeans and similar jacket with front buttons open, alighted. His appearance was casual, but he seemed to be alert and cautious. After the bus left, he looked on both sides of the street as if assuring himself of the solitude, and then quickly began crossing the road directly towards the police station. Ram Singh wondered what could be bringing this man to the police station. Probably a friend or relative of one of the policemen – he thought.

The man suddenly stopped in the middle of the road and looked frightened. It looked as if he was talking to someone. Or rather pleading with some one. He folded his hands, bent down as if trying to touch the feet of some imaginary person and then turned and began running away from the station. And then there were gun shots. From nowhere. The man fell down. Ram Singh felt fear slithering up his spine and sweat over his face, though in his twenty year long service with the police force he had been through several shooting incidents and had handled dead bodies in far worse conditions. The point was that the killer was no where around. The street remained deserted. Not a soul to be seen for hundreds of yards. No one was running away. But some one had shot a man in front of his eyes. And the man was probably dead by now. Riddled with three bullets in his back.

Before Ram Singh could collect his composure, his colleagues came running from inside, "What happened? Where is the firing going on?" The relaxed atmosphere of a few minutes before was suddenly submerged in high degree of tension writ large on each face. Ram Singh was speechless. He pointed towards the dead body and all ran towards it.

Station Incharge Khullar noticed some movement in the pupils of the victim and turned him to bring the face up, brought his ear closer to the lips of the victim and asked, "What happened? Who hit you?" The victim mumbled something. Hardly audible. Something sounded like "edny…. edny arem" and he succumbed.

2

"*Sir jee*," Ram Singh was trying to convince Khullar, "Even if we assume that I had fallen asleep, the full staff of the police station was on the street in a few seconds after the firing and no one saw any one running or any vehicle even though the road was completely deserted for several hundred meters.

"How could any one have run that far in few seconds? Even Milkha Singh can't do that *sir jee!*" He further added.

Khullar could not counter the argument of Ram Singh, but how could the event be explained. How can anyone be shot by no one? Definitely there was someone who immediately hid himself or ran out of sight or escaped in a fast moving vehicle. Probably he came in a fast moving vehicle, shot the victim without coming out or stopping the vehicle and sped away. No other explanation could fit the fact that no vehicle could be seen on the long stretch of the wide straight street where one could spot a vehicle a kilometer away.

But Ram Singh's insistence that the victim stopped in the middle of the street, got frightened, pleaded with some imaginary person and then began running away added inexplicable twists to his theory. Ram Singh was an experienced cop, had a good record and irresponsible statements or observations were not expected from him.

Crime branch had taken charge of the case. They photographed the body from different angles, checked all pockets – interestingly except for the bus ticket and a wallet with 463 rupees in it, nothing was found on the person of the victim. The body was sent for postmortem.

He appeared from a lower middle class background, probably lived alone in Delhi, doing small jobs. May be illegal things. In fact every one believed that the victim was involved in some illegal activities and was killed due to group rivalry. Or probably he was breaking away from a group and threatening to expose it which explained his intended approach to the police station.

The statements of all personnel at the police station were recorded, but the most controversial was Ram Singh's. It was also the most important, he being the only eye witness of the actual incident. But Ram Singh was consistent. He was definitely not under the influence of alcohol or any drugs and was in perfect mental state. His statement still did not make sense.

The last words of the victim also did not make sense. In fact Khullar was not very sure of what exactly he had heard. It sounded like the name of a person. Apparently, moments away from death, the victim was unable to pronounce the name correctly.

Forensic tests will tell more. They had taken a photograph of the victim and flashed it across in all major newspapers to find the identity.

3

The morning chore was done. Sunny was bathed, fed and was now playing on the mat in the small living room with his plastic toys. Babu ji had been sponged and fed his breakfast and was now lying on the bed with closed eyes probably reminiscing his old golden days. Maa ji was sitting next to him on the floor rolling her beads silently, looking clean and satisfied. Sunita herself had also finished her breakfast and now was planning for the lunch silently enjoying the tranquility and the feeling of general contentment prevailing in the atmosphere. The days in Chiragpur were always silent and devoid of any excitement. Activities were confined to repeated cycles of cooking, eating, washing, cleaning, bathing day after day. The old days of scarcity had gone and that was most important. Why should there be any ripples in this serene smooth life now? Things should continue as they are. Slowly Sunny will grow up. Go to school. Get married. And there will be lot of celebration then. Food. Music. Dance. And then there will be a sweet little daughter in law who would take care of Sunita rolling her beads and …

"Didi… didi…" the shrill panicky scream of Mahi, her neighbor and best friend interrupted the flow of Sunita's day dreams. The next moment Mahi was in front of her with a news paper. Visibly upset and badly shaken.

"Look… look didi….it can't be true … it can't be true…" she broke down.

Sunita could not understand any thing. She kept on looking at Mahi with a startled face. Mahi showed her the news paper. There was a photograph and something written below it. Photograph of Pratap, her husband.

Sunita still could not make out what was the matter. But she had clearly understood that whatever it was, was terribly bad. Otherwise why would Mahi be so upset? And why would there be a photograph of her husband in the newspaper.

And then Mahi began trying to explain. "Didi, please see carefully, is this really Pratap bhaiya? I think he just looks like him… he is someone else…."

He certainly looked very much like Pratap. But it can't be him. How can it be him. Only two days ago she had talked to him and he was very fine. He kept on asking about Maaji. He had promised that he would soon be back and then get Babuji treated in Delhi. And about Sunny. He even spoke to sunny when she placed the phone close to his ears. She was dumbstruck, not knowing what to do. Mahi suggested her to call him back and talk. She took out the mobile phone from the bed room and switched on and pressed the call button. She could not understand the recorded message in English and waited to hear the hindi version. Probably the phone was busy. But the message in hindi said the phone was switched off. But this was not unusual. Pratap invariably kept his phone switched off. His job was such. Now what?

Mahi took her phone and began dialing some other number looking at the news paper. And then she kept talking to someone on the phone. She spoke in hindi but Sunita could hear only voices…. voices coming from far and gliding past her and making no sense at all. The world appeared hazy. She had suddenly become oblivious of her surroundings. Enclosed in a cocoon, in her own world, the real world suddenly appeared to be nonexistent. Mahi said something to Maaji, picked up Sunny, caught her hand and almost pulled her to her home next door. Leaving Sunny there with her mother, she again pulled Sunita out, took a rickshaw and left for some place.

They were at the police station. Mahi kept on talking to the Sub inspector. He asked Sunita several things and offered her water. Sunita did not know whether she was answering or whether she drank water. She was still in the cocoon, cut off from the rest of the world. Mahi's father too arrived at the police station, talked to the Sub-inspector for some time, and then they were bundled into a police jeep, which kept on running almost endlessly. They kept on making efforts to talk to Sunita and kept on asking her to drink water from time to time. She looked blankly at them or rather past them, into some distant object through them. She probably answered their questions too, but words never came out of her mouth. The arduous Journey ended a good four hours later at the mortuary in Delhi. The escorting police officer talked to the local police and they were led inside where three wheeled stretchers stood with bodies covered underneath white sheets. The atmosphere reeked of unpleasant formaldehyde and one could feel the silence of death around. They were brought near to one of the stretchers and the police man removed the sheet from the face of the body lying below. Mahi almost screamed and burst into tears. But Sunita said nothing. She was already lying on the dirty, wet floor of the mortuary, unconscious.

4

"Has the lady recovered?' Shiv Prasad asked the Sub-inspector entering the small police office on the ground floor of the government hospital.

"Yes, sir!" The Sub-Inspector answered, "but she is still in deep shock and unable to give any statement or even answer your questions."

"How about her friend and friend's father?"

"They are sitting near her and can be called and questioned."

"Alright then! Let's leave the gentle man with the lady and call her friend. I think the gentle man would in any case not be of much help. He is here only because of his daughter."

A few minutes later Mahi entered the room with eyes still swollen and red.

"I am sorry, Mahi for all that has happened, but to find what happened and why and to be able to find the culprits and get them punished, we need your help." Shiv Prasad said.

Mahi nodded in agreement.

Shiv Prasad pressed the call button beneath his old rexin topped table. A constable immediately entered. Shiv Prasad gave some signal to him and he left.

"Mahi, how do you know Mr. Pratap and Sunita?" Shiv Prasad asked.

"Sunita didi got married a little over one year ago and had come to live in our neighbourhood. Only then we became friends."

"Since when is Pratap living there?"

"Not long ago. His father was working in some company in Bareilly where he got a paralytic attack. After that they all moved to this colony. We don't know much about them – in fact no one knows much about them, because they kept to themselves- they had problems of their own and did not like to mix with others. But they were good, peaceful people. Never had any altercations even among themselves."

"What did Pratap do for a living?"

"I don't know. He was without a job till about four months ago, and did small errands here and there. They were having serious financial problems. Often they went without food but they never complained and never sought help. Only when Sunita didi came, I began talking to her and came to know of their plight."

The constable brought a tray with a glass of water, tea and some biscuits. Shiv Prasad indicated her to have tea. She was feeling exhausted after the long journey and the trauma they were going through. But looking at the biscuits she was reminded of her father and Sunita. Tears came to her eyes again. Shiv Prasad was looking at her. As if he had read her emotions, he told the constable to get some tea and biscuits for her father also, and to inform about the health of Sunita.

Shiv Prasad again turned to Mahi, "What was this job he got in Delhi?"

"I don't know. But it was a good job. Their financial problems were suddenly over and they were happy." Tears again rolled down her cheeks. "Just when things had started to get better, this suddenly happened. God is so unkind sometimes."

Shiv Prasad figured not much could be found from this sweet but dumb little small town girl. Talking to her father would be even more futile. Sunita only would be able to give some good clues. But she would take some more time to recover. Suddenly another question cropped in his mind. "How did Sunita communicate with Pratap? Did he call regularly or did she call him?"

"Pratap bhaiya bought two mobile phones after he got his job. One he left with Sunita and took the other. But they did not talk very frequently." Mahi said.

The constable returned to announce that Sunita was now in a better shape and the doctor has allowed her to be questioned.

Shiv Prasad almost ran upstairs to her bed. Just outside the room the doctor stopped him to tell that though Sunita could be questioned, she was still in deep shock and so he must be very gentle to her.

Shiv Prasad was a veteran in questioning. It was said he could question any one from a four year old to a hardened criminal with equal ease.

Wearing a pleasant smile on his face which did not offend a grieving widow but rather comforted her, he asked Sunita how was she feeling.

She slowly nodded her head sideways indicating ok!

Shiv Prasad pulled a stool near her bed and sat on it, without uttering a word for a few moments as if figuring how to start. Then he suddenly blurted out like some old acquaintance, "He never told you that he was facing a danger?"

Tears welled up her eyes. She shook her head and said, "No. He was quite happy. He told he will come back soon."

"When did he say this?"

"Two days ago, when he called in the evening."

"You remember his phone number? Tell me."

"No, I don't know the number. From my mobile I have to only press one button and that sends the call"

"Ok, let me see your mobile."

"It is at home."

Shiv Prasad was probably having his first encounter with an illiterate pure village girl, who could not even operate a mobile phone. Working out his strategy for further questioning, he asked, "What was his job?" though he was confident this lady won't have an inkling of the job her husband had.

"It was a very good job in Delhi. He travelled to foreign countries and sent lots of money."

Shiv Prasad thought he had got his break. "Oh! How much money did he send, and how?"

"Lots of money. It has filled up my box. I am always scared that thieves may come some day."

"Did he send money orders?"

"No. His friend brought it home. In bags. He said he would come home next week and get Babuji treated in a good hospital."

"Ok! Which countries was he visiting?"

"Foreign. He was travelling in airplanes. I used to see airplanes and imagine that he would be sitting in one of them."

After getting very close to getting answers, Shiv Prasad thought, he was hitting a dead end again.

Leaving Sunita in her bed he came out and found Mahi and her father standing. Her father started, "sahib, Pratap's parents are in Chiragpur so we have to take body there…."

Shiv Prasad understood his contention. He had no money and no resources and wanted help to send the body to Chiragpur. He motioned his Sub-Inspector to take care, and called Mahi again to his little office.

"Mahi, we need the mobile phone of Sunita. It is probably lying at her home. I will send some police constable to their home. Can you please send the message at their home so that they hand it over to the constable?"

Mahi looked a little perplexed. Then took out a phone from her pocket and said, "This is her phone. I took it from her to call Pratap bhaiya after seeing the news of his death."

Shiv Prasad took the mobile, switched on to find that barring the one call to the police headquarters today, all calls were made to or received from only one number – presumably Pratap's!

It was indeed a breakthrough!

5

There was a stunned silence. Shiv Prasad's stare penetrated the eyes deep enough to reach the hearts and brains of the twelve odd police men standing in front of him. But this deep penetrating probe was taking him nowhere.

"I am surprised and shocked to see that some of our colleagues in the police force can be so lowly to steal the cheap mobile phone of a dying person, and more than that, so stupid that they could lift an object which could be a primary evidence in a murder case." He looked around to gauge the effect of his little speech and began again, "Do you know that if you are caught… and believe me, you will be caught…. You too know it very well…. You will be considered an accomplice in this murder…..that is….. even if you are not…."

There was still no reaction. The police men seemed perplexed, but not guilty. Can it be possible that one of these is really an accomplice? Shiv Prasad's stare penetrated Ram Singh's eyes. But there was nothing to read.

Shiv Prasad turned to his Sub Inspector, "call the mobile company again and ask them to check the timings and locations again very very carefully." SI moved to a side to make his call. Shiv Prasad continued his x-ray of the policemen. The SI returned after a few minutes and said, "Sir, they are reconfirming. On 26th January at 15 minutes past 3 PM the mobile phone of Pratap was here at Akbar

Road. It remained here for about ten minutes more and then was switched off a few seconds before 3.25 PM."

"Look boys!" Shiv Prasad's tone was menacing, "This man was murdered at 3.15 PM in front of the police station and before the eyes of constable Ram Singh. No one sees any one. The whole police station runs to the dead body where the man and his mobile are lying but no one sees the mobile! Then ten minutes later, just before the crime branch detectives reach the spot, the phone gets switched off and removed from the spot of crime. Who other than one of the policemen from this station could do this? You guys had apparently cordoned the area and were guarding it then, and no one could have breached your cordon without your help." Shiv Prasad turned to Khullar, "Am I wrong?"

"No, sir!" khullar said, "But I myself was present there and I can confidently say there was no phone there. I myself checked the pockets of the victim in front of all these people."

"OK!" a desparate Shiv Prasad concluded, "Don't confess! We will find the facts the hard way!" He got up and left the police station with his Sub-Inspector.

"When will we have a list of all phone calls from this number?" he asked his SI.

"Sir, by the time we reach office, it should have been faxed to us."

6

Before entering his own cabin, Shiv Prasad peeped into Elizabeth's cabin. She was engrossed in some magazine with a smile spread across her pretty face. She lifted her eyes to see Shiv Prasad and her smile widened even more. "Oh! Good that you have come! I was getting bored without any challenging work!"

But towards the end of the sentence her volume and the lightness of voice tapered off. Shiv Prasad's expression clearly showed that there was serious work ahead. After a silence of a few seconds, she added, this time her voice very business-like, but still with the caring and affectionate touch, "I am sending your strong black coffee and will be there myself in a minute." She pressed the call button for the attendant, took out her notepad and pencil, turned her mobile to silent mode and got up. The attendant appeared at the door and she instructed him to get the "usual" for sir.

As she entered Shiv Prasad's cabin, he was in his standard 'deep thinking' pose - both elbows on the table and palms covering his eyes and forehead. She silently entered the room, pulled a chair on the side of the table, sat down, opened her note pad and began fiddling with the pencil. She very well knew that this position could continue for the better part of an hour or even longer. But she had to sit through it, without making the slightest noise. The door soundlessly opened again and a constable entered with a tray with a coffee mug. The aroma of strong Colombian coffee filled the room.

He placed the mug near the left elbow of Shiv Prasad and gave Elizabeth two sheets of paper. It was a list of phone calls made from a mobile phone. The period covered was about four months. There were about seventy calls either received or made. All were to or from one and only one number. She signaled her approval with her eye movements. The constable left the room as silently as he had come.

Elizabeth began drawing some abstract lines on the half filled page of the note pad. The coffee could get cold but it did not matter. The matter which was churning in Shiv Prasad's head right now was more important. It certainly was related to the strange murder of an unknown person on the Republic Day. Strange because it happened in broad day light right in the heart of the city, in front of the police station and before the eyes of a constable, but no one could see the killer or an escape vehicle. However, the news was not headline, since it appeared to be one of those several isolated cases which frequently take place in the metros. The victim was a 'nobody', no terrorist or other similar links were feared, nothing sensational was found except that it happened on that special day, before the eyes of a cop and in front of a police station in broad day light.

"Hmm…." Shiv Prasad raised his head and looked at Elizabeth. She quickly became alert with her pencil ready to start taking notes. She was looking straight into the eyes of Shiv Prasad, waiting for the first words to come out of his mouth.

"OK! Lets see where we stand." Shiv Prasad said after a few agonizing moments. Elizabeth turned her eyes to the note pad.

"Pratap, a young man from a small town is doing some small errands here and there. He does not have many contacts or a social circle. Family background is poor, but with lots of self-respect, which is usually common in middle class families from rural or semi-rural backgrounds. Such people are more unlikely to be involved in illegal or antisocial activities. However, this guy falls into the trap of a smuggler's gang. Most likely without understanding the implications. How and why he fell into this trap is the first question, but with lower importance."

He paused for a while to organize his thoughts further, and then began again, "But soon after joining the gang he realized his mistake. His conscience would not allow it and so he decided to inform the police." He paused again, and then continued, "Apparently, his movements were being closely monitored, being a fresh recruit. As he was approaching the police station, the person or persons keeping watch decided that he could not be allowed any further freedom, and they eliminated him.

"Question number two is, and that is the most serious question, why no one could notice the killer or the escape vehicle. The post mortem says that he was shot from close range – eight to ten feet, and from a standard revolver, not a crudely locally assembled one. Is someone or some people conniving or hiding something?" He paused again and said, "The mobile phone of the victim was at the site of incidence for ten minutes after the murder, when the entire staff of the police station stood near the body. And then the phone was switched off and removed. But no one notices this. And this is the third question to be answered."

"The staff of the police station do not appear to be involved." He concluded, and then asked "Has the mobile…"

Elizabeth handed him the sheets of paper before he could complete the sentence and said, "This phone was being used only for contacting one person. There were no calls to or from any other number."

Following a few moments of silence, she added, "Sir, it is unlikely that this guy had no contacts. He must be having friends. At least one friend. Some contacts through which he was getting small jobs here and there. And then at least one contact who brought him to this smuggler gang. Some relatives or friends who found his bride for him. Shouldn't we go to Chiragpur and find more about him?"

Shiv Prasad weighed the suggestion in his mind for a while and then said, "Must be. But I have serious doubts if they will be of much help. More so, after seeing this phone call list. He never contacted any of his friends or relatives. Nor did anyone else contact him in four months. Even his wife's mobile had no other calls. They were practically cut off from the entire world. There could be a hundred reasons for that, but for our purpose, it may be irrelevant. How he lived makes one curious, but it ends at just that. How he died is what makes us more concerned."

Silence followed again.

"Pratap must have been in constant touch with some members of the gang – getting instructions, giving reports etc. So he must be having access to another communication device. Most likely another phone. Can we not find that other phone?" Elizabeth asked.

Shiv Prasad gave her an admiring look. Her small inputs like this had helped him many times to get to major conclusions and that's why he always shared his thoughts with her.

Elizabeth began dialing the mobile phone company from her phone. Once her call ended, Shiv Prasad began his monologue again, "The gang was paying him handsome amount. He was also travelling abroad. Carrying what? Narcotics? Gold? Arms? To or from which countries? What was the modus operandi? How was he escaping the customs and security - not only of our own country but of other countries also? He was a green horn and so could have been caught easily. Then, he must have been living somewhere in Delhi. He must have got a passport. Now passport is not a very easy thing to get. He certainly did not have one four months ago when he was in Chiragpur. So he got one issued here and has been travelling abroad. Was there no police verification done? Was it a fake passport? There are several lose threads which need to be followed up. If we just find out where he lived, we may have an answer."

Just then Elizabeth's phone started blinking indicating an incoming call. She answered, listened for a while and then disconnected.

Phone company says it is well nigh impossible to tell whether Pratap carried two mobiles. There would always be several mobiles at one place. If we knew the number, they could tell whether that particular number was usually or most of time near this one. But not vice-versa. Further, this mobile was usually in off position- getting on only to make a call or receive one. But there is one interesting information. Most calls were made when the phone was in Geeta Colony area in Trans Yamuna, East Delhi."

Shiv Prasad's eyes brightened for a moment, but then dimmed again. "It is a very large area with lots of slums and lower middle class tenements. I believe lots of such activities have base there. The information is not much, but it still gives us a much needed clue. Let's start enquiring there."

"In the mean time," he further added, "forward the details of Pratap – photograph, fingerprints etc. - to the Passport Office to find if any passport was issued to him under his own or any other name in the last four months. Though I don't think it was ever issued.

"It is going to be a long drawn battle!" He sighed.

Elizabeth left and Shiv Kumar picked up his coffee mug, which was cold like water by now. He put the mug back from where he had lifted it and pressed the call button for the attendant.

7

Dahiya Lunch Home was not only a lunch home, but a restaurant which served lunch, tea, snacks and dinner. There was nothing which could make it distinct from the thousands of similar restaurants in the city. It provided food to about a hundred clients every day, livelihood to its four employees and enough revenues to the proprietor to maintain a family of eight. The clientele comprised of lower middle class workers from the umpteen shops and factories located nearby, truck and tempo drivers and cleaners, auto rickshaw drivers and the like.

Accommodated in hardly 200 square feet area, the restaurant had a small counter in the front, four tables to seat four each, and then an extremely small kitchen where two cooks and a helper sweated out whole day cooking and cleaning for the nonstop flow of customers. The kitchen had a narrow opening on the back side also which was always kept closed, for behind it ran a very dirty stinking sewer. The restaurant would get filled with this stink as soon as it was opened and the stink would not leave the restaurant for a long time. Still the opening served a very useful purpose. Sanjay Dahiya had trouble walking due to polio. The nearest toilet was almost half a kilometer away and the walk to it was difficult even for a person without constraints. Sanjay would control his bladder until the restaurant was free from guests and then quickly go out, release himself and return and close the door behind allowing as little stink to intrude, as possible.

Leaving aside mobility and the fact that he never liked to study and so could never pass the high school, he had no other constraints or limitations. He was quite content to be managing the Lunch Home sitting at the cash counter. He came exactly at 10 in the morning, parked his three wheeler specially designed for him just opposite to the shop on the other side of the road and then crossed the road to the shop aided with his stick. The side where he parked his three wheeler, was occupied by street vendors. They started arriving soon after Sanjay. One of them, selling ladies' lingerie, used Sanjay's three wheeler for the display of his wares and the inside of the vehicle for storing the packed bundles. In lieu of this usage, he took care of his vehicle all day and cleaned it in the evening before it was time for Sanjay to leave.

Behind this street vendors' market, was a park. The park was not really a park but just some open space where some building material and lots of other waste material had been dumped long ago and never been cleared. No children ever played there. No one used it for a walk either. Nevertheless, it was some open space which made the otherwise highly congested locality a little open. There were a couple of poplar trees in this space and during summers sometimes labourers or hand cart pullers took rest under the shade in the afternoons.

Once settled in his seat behind the counter, Sanjay rarely moved from there until eleven pm, when he had to close the shop. His seat behind the counter gave him a good view of the street, his parked vehicle and the park behind his three wheeler also. He did not have to see much inside the restaurant where the lone waiter handled all clients with ease, indifference and even contempt.

At the usual parking place of his three wheeler, on the parapet of the park, a young man in his early twenties with a blue jeans torn on the knees and a shiny jacket, sat with a black coloured backpack, looking forlorn and lost. The parapet did not have enough space for sitting. The parapet was about ten inches wide and in the middle was the steel grill allowing only about five inches to rest one's butt. Street vendors did however use this narrow space sometimes to rest their tired legs.

This guy was not a vendor. Sanjay asked him to move aside so he could park his vehicle. The guy moved without a word and sat down a few feet from there again in the same style. There was something unusual about him. He did not belong to this place. Probably had come to meet someone. Once on his seat, Sanjay turned to find the young man sitting in the same posture. His employees came. Activities in the kitchen began. And then came the first customers for tea and snacks. Sanjay forgot about the guy sitting on the parapet. But after about a couple of hours when he glanced at that side, he was surprised to see him still sitting there. Now he looked at him more carefully. He was certainly tired and hungry. His lips had dried and he was every now and then glancing towards the lunch home. He does not have money, can't beg, and does not know what to do. A confused and lost person. Most likely a student runaway from his home. Sanjay concluded.

He sent his waiter to call him. The young man came and stood timidly in front of Sanjay. Sanjay ran his glance from top to bottom, and was assured that his conclusion was correct. "Are you hungry?" he asked without any prologue.

"Yes" a very low voice, supported with a nod of the head.

"Chhotu, give him food." Sanjay directed his waiter.

The man did not need any further invitation. He, without even thanking Sanjay, came in and took a seat.

"What will you have?" asked Chhotu.

The man hesitated a little, looked at Sanjay as if to gauge what was allowable. Sanjay was looking at him only. He said, "Whatever he wants to eat, give him."

The man now looked at the menu painted on the wall of the restaurant, and said, "Chicken Masala and butter naan."

Chhotu looked back at his master. This was the most expensive dish on the menu, and from what he had understood, this client was not going to pay. Sanjay too looked a little shocked, but indicated him to take the order.

The man had probably not eaten for a couple of days. He ate voraciously and without any hesitation. Chhotu would look back at his master every time he was to bring another naan, but Sanjay appeared to be in a very generous mood today.

The man's appearance took a very different shape after he had eaten. The tired, anguished and forlorn look was almost gone. He came to the counter. Still did not thank, but said, "Sir, I don't have a home or a job. I am willing to work. Can you give me a job?" He spoke fluent English, which Sanjay was not able to do. He was impressed to some extent. He asked him to sit down on a chair near the counter and began talking to him.

The guy's name was Ankit. He was undergoing some professional course in down south, but was not really interested in it. He did not like south at all and wanted to live in north, where he had grown up, particularly Delhi. His parents were not his real parents and so would not care for his feelings. He had finally decided to leave everything and try his luck. He appeared intelligent and Sanjay was wondering why parents do not care for their only child. He too did not like to study, but his parents understood his feelings and did not press him to pass those exams. His dad helped him take over this shop and now all of them were happy. He offered to call his parents and explain them his feelings so that he could return to his own home, and things could be alright. But Ankit dissuaded him. There was no point in doing so, They won't understand! He was firm in his resolve.

But Sanjay had no place to accommodate him. He lived in a two bedroom flat with his parents, grand mother, a brother looking for a job, a bhabhi, a one year old niece and a twenty year old sister. There was too little space for themselves. He could not give him a job either. But he was very sympathetic towards him and wanted to help. At last he asked Chhotu to see if he could accommodate him in their home till the time his problems were sorted out. All his employees ate at the Lunch home only and this one addition would be no real burden.

Chhotu and the three other employees of Dahiya Lunch Home shared a 150 square foot room with two more students about a kilometer from the restaurant. The room was small enough for six. But the four employees warmly welcomed Ankit to their 'sweet home' after hearing his story. They slept on the floor on thin cotton mattresses laid next to each other. Inclusion of another person did not require addition of a mattress – in fact there was no space to lay another mattress – but just squeezing oneself a little more. In winters, it is better that we sleep closer – we will be warmer – they joked. During day time they would roll all the bed material and clean up the room to sit and gossip. The students studied in this room during day, if they did not have classes.

Chhotu escorted Ankit to their home, introduced him to the students and leaving him there, went back to the restaurant. Ankit talked to the students for some time and then fell asleep. He did not wake up till late next morning.

8

When he woke up, the room was vacant. He looked around. There was a small slip of paper near his pillow. He took it. Someone had scribbled in hindi that there was some milk in the sauce pan which he could heat and drink. If he had to go out, he could leave the keys with anyone of Lunch home staff. He looked around again. There was no furniture. One side was the lone window and another side the door. Near the door were some pairs of badly worn bathroom slippers and one pair of sports shoes. The walls had nails driven in and lots of clothes hung from these nails. Whatever was left of the walls was covered with posters of hindi film actresses in least possible clothes. On one side also hung a framed picture of Vaishno Devi. On the frame left-overs of burnt out incense sticks were still stuck. Three ramshackle suitcases lied in one corner. On the suitcases lied more clothes. On one suitcase lied several toothbrushes, a small tube of toothpaste, two open plastic soap cases with wafer thin pieces of soaps, one blue coloured detergent bar wrapped in paper and a small mirror. Next to these suitcases was an electric heater and on it was the saucepan. There were two steel glasses and five small glasses in which usually the roadside stalls serve tea. All had some remnants of tea at the bottom.

He looked inside the saucepan. There was some milk in it. But it did not look inviting enough. He put the lid back and returned to his original position. He was not sure what he wanted to do. He kept sitting for a while. Then got up, and went out of the room. It was already well past into the day. Must be around noon. He thought.

The common toilet was slightly away. There was also a washbasin outside the toilet and a miniscule piece of soggy red coloured soap lied there. The toilet stank. He stood on the doorway, unzipped his jeans and relieved himself. Without flushing he returned to his room.

A middle aged man soon entered the room. Looked at him not in a friendly way, and demanded, "Who are you? How did you come here?"

Ankit got scared. He fumbled for an answer, and then said, "I am a new employee at the Dahia lunch Home. My duty will begin in a few hours."

"You can't live here. If you want to live here, you will also have to pay Rs. 300 every month."

"OK. I will pay." Ankit promised.

"No. You have to pay one month's advance and also give me your police verification. Rules are very strict for paying guests."

"But I don't have money now. I will pay when I get my salary." Ankit pleaded.

"In any case these boys should have told me before hand if they were subletting it. Subletting is not allowed. They are making a fool of Harshu bhaiya? Let them come in the evening. I will kick each one out. Tell them to meet me whenever they come. Understand?"

Ankit nodded, hoping that the ordeal had ended. The man turned to go back, but again turned to face Ankit, "And you don't know how to use the bathroom? You don't know how to use the flush? Have you come from a village?"

"But I flushed…" Ankit said.

"Don't lie. No one tells lies to Harshu Bhaiya. Go and flush now or I will throw you out."

Ankit rushed out to implement the orders. But the toilet did not have a flush. It only had a plastic mug. Ankit looked back. Harshu Bhaiya stood behind him. Ankit quickly filled the mug with water and poured the water into the pan.

"Wash properly. You peed from here and have soiled the entire floor." Harshu Bhaiya shouted.

Ankit filled up again and threw the water on the floor. After pouring four mugs, when he looked back again, there was no one. He sighed with relief and went back to his room.

He was beginning to feel hungry again.

He went to the suitcase, picked up the mirror and looked at himself. He had not shaved for days. He looked around the suitcases and found a used throw-away safety razor. He picked up the mirror, the razor and the soap case and went to the wash basin. Applied soap to his face and began shaving. After a few minutes his appearance had definitely improved over what it had been a few minutes ago. He took out a comb from his pocket, combed his hair and looked at himself with satisfaction. He took everything back into the room, left them on the suitcase, put on shoes, picked up his back pack, took the keys and went out after locking the door.

He reached the Dahiya Lunch Home and greeted Sanjay with a smile and a loud Hi!

Sanjay returned the smile, "You slept too much."

"Yes I had been travelling for the past four days and had practically not slept. Now after this sleep I am feeling fresh."

"What is the plan for today?"

"I will eat something and then go out – look for a job."

Sanjay's heart skipped a beat....again that sumptuous meal without a payment? But it would be impolite to deny food to a hungry and desolate man. He wisely instructed Chhotu to serve Ankit some daal and roti.

Ankit sat down at the table, but as Chhotu brought daal and two rotis, he pleaded, "Bhaiya, a little bit of chicken too. I can't eat with daal alone."

Both Chhotu and Sanjay were flabbergasted at the audacity of this uninvited self imposing guest. Chhotu looked back at Sanjay for instructions. Sanjay rummaged for the right response for a moment and then signaled him to go ahead. Ankit happily started without noticing the reactions of his hosts, though he was sitting with his face towards the entry and so facing Sanjay.

Hardly had he started that a young foreigner couple approached the Lunch Home. Delhi does not have a dearth of foreigners, but hardly anyone ever came to this side of the city. The couple was in their mid twenties. The man wore a dirty light coloured trouser and a jacket fully open from the front. His thin off-white shirt too had most of its buttons open, exposing his bare chest with some hair in the middle. He had a large back pack, which probably carried the entire luggage of the couple. The girl had a Rajasthani style skirt and top which they must have bought a few days ago at Janpath or Connaught Place. Necklaces with small and large beads from a similar source adorning her neck were visible in spite of the brown coloured sweater wound round her neck. She had a smaller back pack and a bottle of water.

Sanjay was overjoyed to imagine that a foreigner couple was coming to have lunch at his restaurant. The man asked something from Sanjay. Sanjay did not understand any english any way and with the unfamiliar accent of this foreigner he was completely at a loss. But the opportunity was not to be lost. He immediately said, "Yes, sir! Good non-vegetarian food, sir. Very cheap and tasty. Please come, sir!"

The man started again, "No, I don't want food….."

Ankit quickly swallowed the big piece of roti he had just stuffed in his mouth, left his seat with his fingers still greasy with chicken curry, and coming to the counter asked in chaste English, "How may I help you, Sir?"

The couple was relieved to find someone who could speak good English. Both looked at him admiringly. The man showed a piece of paper and said, "I need to go to this address, but don't have a clue as to where it could be."

"Certainly I can help you, sir!" Ankit said, ran to the wash basin at the end of the shop, washed his hands, picked up his backpack and returned with the swiftness of a squirrel. He pulled the slip from the man's hand and said, "Come, I will show you." Without bothering to even take a look at what was written on it he began leading them in one direction.

More than disappointment of losing the opportunity of having a foreign client, Chhotu and Sanjay were envious of Ankit stealing the show. Chhotu shouted from behind, "Oye, finish your lunch at least, it may be free for you, to us it costs money."

But Ankit did not even look back, he just waived behind himself which could either mean that he would return soon or he may not return at all and they could dispose off his leftover lunch.

Ankit took them to the next lane where the prying eyes of Sanjay or Chhotu could not reach. Now he unfolded the slip of paper and read. It was some address. Ankit was as alien to this area as these foreigners and had no inkling whether this address belonged to this part of the city or elsewhere.

Asking them to wait for a moment he went to another shop nearby and asked about the address. The shop attendant indicated him the way – to go to this place, he would have to again cross Dahiya Lunch Home and then walk for about ten minutes.

He insisted, "Is there no way from this side?"

"It will be much longer and very bad approach. That side is cleaner. You will reach in ten minutes."

But Ankit had no intention of crossing the Lunch home where Sanjay or Chhotu could snatch his opportunity. He began walking in the other direction – the longer and dirtier approach. At the same time he began conversation with the couple. "The people here are very cunning. They may tell you the wrong way. They will pretend to be helping you even if they neither can help nor have any intention of helping. You must be very careful of such people. They may even dupe you."

"We have been lucky so far! Everyone we met had only been helping really!" The girl said with a smile.

"What is your name?" Asked Ankit

"I am Katerina and he is Peter." The girl said.

"Oh! Are you from Russia?" Ankit seemed excited.

"No! We are from Romania! There are similar names in Russia and Romania!" The girl said.

"Actually I have travelled to Russia. I have been planning to visit Romania too, very soon."

"Is it? Where do you want to go in Romania?" asked Katerina.

Ankit was now cornered. He did not even know its capital city. But he was smart in talking, "I haven't decided yet. I think in a couple of months I will decide. If you leave me your address, I will contact you when I go there."

"Yes, it will be good to see you there!" Katerina said, but did not make any move to share her address.

"Just a minute." Said Ankit and went to another shop to again ask the address.

Then they kept moving straight and after about two hundred metres took a left turn in to a very narrow lane, a quarter of which was a drain full of papers, leaves, plastics, vegetable and fruit peels and the like.

"See, there are no road signs, names or directions. Roads are so dirty. A foreigner can easily get lost here." Ankit said as if talking to himself. No one commented.

"What brought you to India?" Ankit tried to restart the conversation.

"It is a lovely country. We had been reading about its mysteries and charms and wanted to see it for ourselves." Said Peter, "What do you do?"

"I have just finished my Hotel Management course and am now looking for a job. I have offers from some very good properties in Delhi, Mumbai and Goa, but I would prefer to work abroad. How is the hotel industry in Romania?"

"Really can't say! Peter said, "There are many hotels and good luxury ones also. But I know nothing about their business." He laughed.

They again turned left and were now on the same road on which about a hundred meters away stood Dahiya Lunch Home. But now they were walking away from that Lunch Home. "Isn't it the same place from which we came?" recognizing the road, Katerina asked.

Ankit thought he was caught, so quickly changed the topic, "You are looking for some particular person or some office or institute?"

They both exchanged glances. Peter hesitated for a moment and then said, "We need to meet this man- we have a common friend in Romania."

"Where are you staying in Delhi? If you need more help I can certainly come there."

"We keep changing!" Peter said, pointing to his backpack, "See, we move with the entire luggage and wherever we feel like stopping, we stop!"

"How long are you going to be in Delhi?"

"Don't know again!" He laughed. We may leave in ten minutes or may stay ten days!" He did not want to give straight answers to Ankit.

First time during this walk they came across a road name. Ankit checked the address on his slip and took them left again. Incidentally, some of the houses had numbers written on them. Ankit could finally guess which house they wanted. He went to that door and knocked.

"Who is it?" Voice came from inside.

Ankit did not know what to say. He looked at the couple.

"Say friends." Katerina said.

But before Ankit could say anything, the door opened and a middle aged man appeared looking at them questioningly.

"These people are from Romania. They wanted to see Mr. Duke." Ankit said.

"Who has sent you?" The man directed his question towards the couple.

They exchanged glances as if deciding whether to tell or not. The man waited for a moment and then asked Peter to come along and others to wait there. He came out of the house and with Peter moved further away on the same road.

"Which other places did you visit in India?" Ankit did not want the conversation to end.

"We visited Taj Mahal and Jaipur. Now we intend to go to Goa later this week."

"Oh! I could help you around in Kerala. I have some friends there who can arrange your stay and sightseeing at a very low budget. When are you planning to go there?"

Katerina was not keen on continuing this discussion. She looked at her watch and asked, "Where has he taken him? Why is it taking so long?" About ten minutes had passed so her concern was genuine.

"Perhaps Duke's house is on that side. He wants to confirm." Ankit said, "Do not worry, I am with you, nothing will happen." But Ankit himself was more scared than Katerina. He had not at all liked the look of the person.

"Do you think I can find a job in Romania" Ankit started again.

"I am not sure." She said, "May be. You will have to try."

Few more minutes passed and then at the far end of the road they could see Peter and the man coming. Ankit suddenly got relaxed. Happily he pointed at them, "See! I told you nothing will happen! Here he is coming back!"

Peter came and signaled to Katerina that all was well. He took out a hundred rupee note and gave it to Ankit, "Thanks for all the trouble!"

"Thank you! Sir! If you need more help, please remember you have a friend here!"

But the couple had already walked away.

Ankit happily pocketed the money and began to walk back. After a few steps, he stopped and turned in the direction away from Dahiya Lunch Home. A few hundred meters away he found another restaurant, slightly better than Dahiya Lunch Home, and entered with a confidence on his face. He ordered Chicken Masala and Naan and sat down like a busy man relaxing after a hard day. After finishing the lunch, when he went to the counter, he was given a bill of rupees 116. Suddenly his confidence and the air of superiority he was wearing for about an hour, was lost. The forlorn and dejected look returned and he started pleading again with the cashier to forgive him because he had only hundred rupees.

9

The atmosphere in Geeta Colony police station was in total contrast to Akbar Road Police station. It was small, dirty and very crowded. At any point of day or night some complainants would be sitting on the benches in the outer office waiting for their turn. Invariably a drunk would be caught, locked up for the night and then released the next day after the next of kin paid for this hospitality. But sometimes no one came looking for the person and then the police station staff got worried about how to get rid of the person.

Then there were umpteen roadside scuffles, eve teasing, minor accidents, thefts etc and each of these incidents brought in cash from both sides – the complainant and the accused. The real art was to get the most from both sides without really doing anything for either of them. Now the Station House Officer or the SHO, was sitting with his two assistants in his cabin. They did not get along very well, but on many issues like extracting the most from their 'clients' and avoiding the work assigned by their seniors, their views were similar.

"Crime branch wants us to find the house of this dead man!" SHO sneered.

"Sister f***ers" his assistant grimaced, "What makes them think that he lived here."

"Astrology dear.... Astrology" commented the second assistant, "It is easy for them to transfer their responsibilities to police stations and then close the case after some time putting the blame on us!"

"The Enquiry Officer is Shiv Prasad. He will ask for a report every day and make our life hell." SHO did not make an attempt to hide his anguish at this unnecessary work being loaded upon them, but had no options other than to start acting on it.

"We have to do something about it." He said.

"Nothing ji, nothing!" the second assistant was still nonchalant, "Let's also do what they have done….. give this work to Pandit. Shiv Prasad can keep taking his reports five times a day from him!"

All three of them laughed and immediately agreed on this bright idea. SHO called his attendant and asked to send Constable Pandit.

"Pandit won't be found anywhere, sir!" The attendant said, "He would be at some desi daru joint if he has already not fallen into a sewer."

"Find him out and send him immediately. This is urgent. Headquarter's orders." SHO said.

The Attendant went out cursing. He almost exactly knew where Pandit would be found, but did not want to go there. Now he had no options. Headquarter's orders!

It was the first floor corner of a three story building which had remained un-constructed for several years after casting of the floor slabs of the three floors. Now it looked dilapidated. Moss had gathered on all edges of the concrete slabs. The stairs were full of empty cigarette packets and butts, broken glass bottles and even excreta. But this one corner was the favorite of most drunkards of the colony. No one disturbed them here. They also had a roof above them so after getting too high, they could also lie down to sleep.

No one needed company here. As soon as they could lay their hands on a bottle, they rushed to the spot and enjoyed themselves. Singing, shouting, sleeping! If someone joined, then the two would do the same things together, otherwise alone. Sometimes larger groups formed and then there would be discussions on every conceivable topic of the world. But usually these people preferred to shout out aloud expletives for their bosses, neighbours, wives or anyone else who had been advising them to stay away from liquor.

As he had guessed, Pandit was at this usual haunt. With three more persons in similar state. Pandit was the current speaker. Others did not seem to be paying any attention to him. But that was no deterrence.

The Attendant came close to him and shouted, "Pandit, SHO saheb wants you at the Police Station. Immediately."

"Look! What did I say?" Pandit began his address though no one seemed to be listening, "Without me they cannot live even five minutes. As soon as I come out the SHO begins to fret. All important and dangerous work is assigned to me. But when it comes to promotion, they forget my name."

He turned to the Attendant and in an authoritative tone, said, "Go and tell him I am coming."

"No telling business." Attendant quipped, "he wants me to bring you with me. Come at once."

Pandit continued his curses but started to get up. He took a good five minutes to get up and start moving.

Ten minutes later they were in front of the SHO. "Salam Saheb." Pandit gave his drunken salute and stood blinking his eyes.

"You again started drinking during duty hours?" SHO roared.

"No sir! I swear upon my son!" Pandit pleaded, "Haven't touched liquor. I was on guard duty outside the Shiva temple." He paused to look at his reaction then added, "haven't touched liquor for months."

"Yes, that is very visible." Said an annoyed SHO. Then handed him over a sheet carrying a photograp, "look carefully at this man."

Pandit folded and kept the sheet in his pocket, "Don't worry, sahib! By evening I will deliver him here."

"No. You can't deliver him." SHO said, "You have to find out where he lived."

"Done sir!" Pandit was relieved to be released do easily, "I will bring him here – you can ask him his entire history and geography!" He had still not bothered to take a look at the photograph. But then even the SHO was not bothered. The buck had been passed. Duty over. It did not matter whether Pandit knew that this man was living or dead. He was any way unlikely to do anything!

As soon as he came out of the police station, he was back to his original self. He began cursing the SHO for calling him back to the police station and spoiling his fun. The whole effect of his liquor had vanished and he would have to take some more. He headed straight to the nearby liquor shop which sold country liquor.

10

After some argument, Ankit was allowed to go without having to pay the balance 16 rupees.

He came out of the restaurant. Began walking in one direction without any particular destination or objective in mind. He had sumptuous lunch and now had nothing to worry about in the world. Katerina had been very nice to him. She had probably begun to like him. She was only scared of her boy friend. If he was not there, he could have befriended her more. She said it would be nice to see him in Romania. But she did not give her address. If she had, he would have travelled to Romania and then they could live happily ever after!

He kept walking for about half an hour without going anywhere in particular when suddenly he heard a voice calling him. He looked around. There was no one. He thought it was an illusion and moved again. But the voice came again, "Ankit".

He stopped again, looked around and then got a little scared. He had been told by a psychiatrist that he was mildly schizophrenic. And he had searched about this in the internet. Schizophrenics heard sounds. He had never heard any sounds. But then, he was only mildly schizophrenic. Now probably it was getting stronger and he had begun to hear voices. He decided to ignore it and move on. But the voice came again. It was clear and certainly not an illusion.

"I am you inner voice, Ankit!" It said.

He had been told by his father several times to listen to his inner voice and do the right things. But he had never heard this voice earlier. And now this inner voice had got activated. It was talking to him. And talking in clear, very crisp voice.

He stood there waiting for the voice to say something again. And it did not disappoint him.

"Turn left and keep moving." It said. Ankit followed. The voice kept moving with him continuously talking to him, "You are born to do great things. You should not be roaming around on streets like this. You should be moving in Ferraris. Travelling round the globe. Living a rich stylish and glamorous life. Do not waste your time on this street. Fortune is waiting for you. I will guide you to your fortune."

The voice kept on guiding him and brought to a decent looking apartment building. It further guided him through the stairs and to a particular apartment. As he stood there, the voice said, "From now on, this apartment is yours. You are the owner of this house."

Another sound of someone walking up the stairs came and the voice became silent. Ankit was eager to hear more but it remained silent until the coming man walked past them and had entered one of the apartments on the higher floor. Ankit silently waited for the voice. It came again, "Look at the stairs going up - on the third step on the left hand side is a key. This is the key to your apartment. Come on, open the door and get in. Ankit saw. Indeed there was a key on the third step. He picked it up. He was apprehensive of trying to open the door. Will it not be a break-in? He had never indulged in illegal activities. He stood still with the key in his hand.

"I told you this is your house." The voice came again, "Do not hesitate. Open the lock."

Ankit moved forward and with trembling fingers turned the key in the lock. The door opened. He pushed it open and stood watching.

"Move in Ankit," His inner voice said, "You should never hesitate to enter your own house." The sound was mellow and comforting.

He moved in. The apartment was nicely furnished. The living room had a sofa set, a home theatre and a small dining table with four chairs.

The inner voice guided him to the bed room. There were two bed rooms, with clean queen size beds.

Ankit was suddenly shocked and scared. In one of the bed rooms on a side table lied an AK47 assault rifle. He had till now seen these rifles in movies or hanging from the shoulders of police personnel. A rifle lying unattended so close to him and in the so called his own apartment was terrifying. He never liked real life fights. If someone challenged him on a road, he just gave in without putting up even a mild protest. He had never thought of harming a mouse even. But now an AK47 was on the side of his bed. He was looking at it with apprehension. The inner voice came to his rescue. "Do not get alarmed. It is for self defence only. You need not touch it at all. May be you can keep it in one of your cupboards, hidden from sight and forget all about it."

Ankit relaxed a bit, but not enough.

The inner voice came again, "You will find everything you may need. There is a fridge in the kitchen. Quite a few things are already there. But if you don't want any of those, just check your cupboards – there is a lot of money in one of them. Its all yours. You may go out and have the best food in town.

Ankit moved forward and opened a cupboard. Inside was a small locker. It was not locked. He opened it. The inner voice was correct. It was full of currency notes. Several hundreds. No. Several thousands. Perhaps lakh. It was difficult to believe his ears till now. Now it was difficult to believe his eyes too. Probably it was a dream. In a few minutes he would wake up and find himself in the train he had been travelling for the past so many days. Or the bench on the platform. At best in the small stinking dungeon those boys called home.

The inner voice began again, "Ankit, this all is yours. But you have to keep it safe. You are a rich man now. And the poor keep trying to rob the rich. There is a good possibility that some thieves may break in. They may try to take away all of your money. The money God has given you today. You must save it. You must save yourself. You have a right to live happily forever. And you must not allow anyone to snatch this right from you." The inner voice paused, and then restarted, "Come back to the living room."

He went back to the living room.

"Look, here on this table is a revolver."

Indeed there was a revolver. Surprisingly, he had not noticed it when they entered the room first. It was lying so openly and was so prominently visible that no one in the room could have ever missed it lying on this table. However, he had not seen it earlier.

"This is yours. Don't get scared. You have to protect yourself. Keep this revolver under your pillow every night. There may be thieves coming in the night. If you see any one, do not hesitate. Just point the revolver at him and shoot. And shoot again and again till the bullets run out. This man must not be left alive. He must not escape. Anyone trying to harm you or take your wealth away, has no right to live. Just point the revolver and start shooting at him. You will be safe and will enjoy all your wealth rest of your life."

The inner voice kept on repeating the same words in different tones and scales again and again. Finally it said. "Okay. Hide the revolver under pillow. Take some money out of the safe and go out and have some good dinner. But come back before late, lock the door and sleep peacefully."

Ankit was not very comfortable picking up the revolver, but he could not defy the inner voice. He picked it up. It was heavy. Unlike his toy pistols. He took it to his bed room and hid under the pillow. He opened the cupboard and the locker and took out several hundred rupee notes. Armed with money, he moved towards the main door, picked up the keys, opened the door and came out. After coming out he looked all around cautiously. He was scared of the thief. But there was no one around. He closed the door and locked it. Then he moved out. Lot more confident and joyous.

He did not know where he wanted to go. It was evening. After walking for a few minutes he found an auto rickshaw. Got in and ordered him to drive to Connaught Place.

He spent quite some time walking in Connaught Place and then walked into an expensive bar cum restaurant.

11

Rocky was terribly tired. For the last three days he had been on the dirty narrow lanes and bylanes of Geeta Colony without any success. He had been ditched by his own men. Not that he trusted them very much, but he sure did not expect them to leave him in a lurch like this. His carefully chalked out program was ruined. This small operation could have brought him a billion dollars and he could lead a very happy peaceful life without ever having to do anything in life. But his stupid assistant developed cold feet at the last hour. The advance payment of hundred million dollars had been received by him and the payer would demand to know when the work would be completed. Failure in the first promised operation, which he had assured them, had no reason to fail, had eroded his credibility considerably.

What was worse, was that the whole story was about to be released to the police. Catching him even then would have been impossible, but Rocky did not want to take such risks. The scoundrel had to be eliminated. He had very smartly traced him, followed him and finally been able to eliminate him. This was a great risk again. His closely guarded secret could have been found. But he had acted smart. No one could guess what had happened. Had there been any other constable, everyone would have thought that the constable had killed him. Constable Ram Singh had such a good record and was respected so much that this possibility was not being talked about.

Taking advantage of the shock and confusion, he had also cleverly taken away the mobile phone and the key of the apartment from his pockets and moved away before the posse of police men reached the victim. Unfortunately before dying the scoundrel spoke out his nick name, but the dumb police would probably never make out anything out of those syllables.

Leaving him there, he had set out to find Bhure lal, the second assistant. It was very clear to him that after seeing such an end of his friend, Bhure Lal would quickly run away and if he too had the audacity like Pratap, would report the matter to police. The good part was that none of them knew almost anything about him, but they knew the contacts and could put the contacts in trouble. And that would be very very detrimental to his business. To his source of income. He would have to rebuild the contacts again. But this is a small world. His failure and the consequences of that failure would be known to the entire underworld in no time and no one would easily do any business with him. No. This was too big a risk. The other scoundrel also had to be eliminated.

He immediately left out for Geeta Colony where the duo shared this apartment. But Bhure Lal had already left the apartment. He had stealthily entered the apartment using Pratap's key, and guessed that Bhure had not taken anything out of the apartment. He would certainly come back to collect at least part of the money. It was a lot of money to be left. The point was how long would he wait. He would definitely not go to his family or to Pratap's family for he could be easily caught there. He must be hiding some where in Geeta Colony. May be with one of the distributors. And would return as soon as he thought the danger had subsided. But he was running out of patience, strength, and worst of all, time.

Bhure was to carry the material to Italy and deliver it there. Since Bhure had now abandoned him. This would have to be done by himself. He did not want to get involved in these small dealings, but with the major contract failing due to Pratap developing cold feet, he had no option but to keep these smaller dealings alive. At least until the major contract was executed successfully. And that may take an year. Similar opportunity won't come earlier.

After following up all the dealers and other smaller contacts in Geeta Colony for three days, he was getting panicky. He had no assistants who could be trusted to do this job. And then he saw this young man accompanying the East European couple asking for the address of Duke. Duke was one of his retailers. Bhure Lal could very well be hiding in his house. Rocky followed them. Though he could not find Bhure Lal, watching Ankit for some time and hearing his conversation with them he was convinced that the man was slightly deranged mentally. Seeing his behavior after getting a hundred rupee note, he became sure that he could be easily led to believe anything and to do anything. And he had no contacts too. He was living a homeless vagabond's life. Living off whatever he could lay his hands on.

He conceived the plan instantly. He made the man believe that he was his inner voice and was out to help him lead a good life. Now this man would be living in the apartment, ready to shoot the intruder, as soon as one entered. And the second bird would also be killed with this one stone. The weapon used in Pratap's murder would be with this man. So the second murder would also stand solved. God willing, by the time he returned from Italy, Bhure would have left for his heavenly abode and this stupid guy would have landed in the lock up facing trial for the two murders.

He came out of the metro and began walking towards Hotel le Meridien. He had almost no strength left but had to make the effort. Any way after a few minutes he would be resting in his hotel room and would be fresh by tomorrow to take that arduous flight.

At the entrance of the hotel several security guards stood in smart uniforms. Several guests stood waiting for their cars to come. The entry to lounge could be only through the door frame metal detector. All luggage had to pass through an X-ray.

Hotels have also become airports! Laughed Rocky in his heart. But the security arrangements at all the five star hotels are more of ornamental value. The security guards appeared to be very alert and thorough, but in effect, they were amateurs. Actually, carrying out a really serious checking would certainly inconvenience the guest and they may get annoyed. In hospitality industry, that would be the last thing any entrepreneur would want. So the solution was to put up a great show of perceived security. Crossing this security was a child's play for Rocky.

He waited for a few minutes, then walked past the space on the side of the metal detector door frame. A girl talking on her mobile was entering the lobby through the revolving glass door. He followed her through this revolving door and was in the lobby. He sat down on a single chair lying near a pillar, intently watching the entry to the washrooms.

He saw a man with a walking stick moving towards the washroom. He followed him and as soon as he entered the washroom, he too entered, and stood silently in a corner.

The man relieved himself, washed his hands and walked out. There was no one in the washroom. Rocky felt his left wrist, took out a golden metal band with several red, green and yellow stones from his left wrist, watched it admiringly for a while and then over himself. He was looking at himself after three days.

The memory of that day about two years ago flashed in his mind, bringing a very satisfying smile even in this condition.

....

They were celebrating their graduation. A friend had arranged a luxury yacht. About twenty of them, boys and girls, were on the yacht. The yacht had everything on board - lots of booze and food, games. After some time they stopped in the middle of the sea to try their hands at fishing. They picked up fishing rods and spread out on different sides of the yacht. Rocky was actually a misfit in the group. His middle class background created a kind of wall between himself and his friends. But he enjoyed the flamboyant life style of the spoilt offsprings of the rich and super rich. He always somehow managed to get into their company and parties. The contempt sometimes became too evident but in order to enjoy this lifestyle he suppressed his self esteem and continued their company. Today while every one was on the main deck and enjoying everything else more than fishing, he moved to the backside which was at the lowest level, close to the sea. He tried for about ten minutes without success and then lost interest. He thought of finding the depth of water at that place and began rolling out the fishing line. The whole line was unwound but he did not get any idea whether the bait had touched the floor of the ocean or not. He waved the rod but no indications still. Finally he began pulling out.

As the bait surfaced, he was amazed to find a shiny little thing stuck in it. He took it in his hands. It was a golden wrist band, impregnated with coloured stones. He was about to shout and draw attention of his friends but stopped immediately. It could be a very precious thing. Why share it? He hid it in his pocket and did not tell anyone about it.

Later in his room in the evening, he took it out and inspected again. He couldn't tell whether the stones were precious or not. He could not even say if it was real gold or some ordinary yellow metal. But it was shining brightly. The sea had not corroded or faded its glow. Hence it must be expensive. He concluded.

He tried it on his wrist and to his horror saw his arm disappearing. He touched it with his right hand and couldn't see his right hand either. He was scared. He looked all over himself and could not see himself. He ran to the mirror but could not see anyone in the mirror also. He was petrified. Was he dead? He wanted to shout but the voice seemed to have been choked out of fear. But how could he be dead, he was able to see everything else, the bed, the lamp, the chair, the mirror, but not himself in the mirror! After some time he could collect his wits and felt his left wrist again. He could feel the wrist band. He pulled it out and saw himself return in the mirror. He was amazed. He tried it several times. Every time he put on the band on his left wrist, he disappeared and re-appeared when he took it out. It was great fun.

He came out of his room and went into the living room. His parents were watching TV and discussing something. They did not seem to notice him. He touched a flower vase on the side table near his dad. It fell and broke. Ma was annoyed. "Why can't you sit without moving all round?" she shouted at Dad.

"But I did not even touch it!" Dad pleaded.

"Oh, then a ghost came and felled it!" Ma said sarcastically.

"Ghost or whatever" Dad was both annoyed and surprised, "I swear, I did not touch it."

None of them were even looking at Rocky who stood next to the side table. Apparently, they were not able to see him. Rocky was elated. He went back to his room and hid the band in his cupboard between the clothes. This gadget would be great fun! He thought.

Next morning he very innocently asked Dad how the vase broke, and Dad once again expressed his surprise. "There was no wind, no earthquake, no mice, and I did not touch it. But it fell on its own. Your mum doesn't believe it. Even I don't believe it, but that's exactly what happened."

Rocky said, "I don't believe in ghosts. But is there any gadget which can make a person disappear? Let's say someone stood here and felled it!"

Dad laughed out aloud and addressed Ma, "Hey! Listen, I know how the vase broke! You remember when we were young that story was making rounds about a man disappearing! That man had come and broken this vase!"

Ma too laughed recalling the old story. "Yes! How the hype was created. There were even stories that the man busted a terrorist gang! But later all that subsided."

"Yeah it all became silent after some time. For a few months all news papers screamed only about 'Mr. India' Yes, this guy was calling himself Mr. India!"

"I think it was one of those magicians like PC Sorcar, taking their tricks to the street."

"So many such things keep happening. Sometimes deities start drinking milk, dead come back to life…… You remember, one guy had claimed that he could turn water to petrol…."

Their discussions went on but Rocky had found what he wanted to find. There had been such a gadget and somehow it reached the bottom of the sea. Stories that dad was talking about may not be all wrong. He also realized the potential this gadget carried. If he played his game well, he could soon be the strongest, the richest person on earth, and he could then return the contemptuous looks and treatment of his friends with interest!

………………………

He had started developing his plans and within two years had reached such a high stage, so close to his goal! He kissed the band, kept it in his pocket and reached the wash basin to have a good look at himself. He wore a forlorn look. Unshaved, unkempt, dirty. Thanks to the arduous three night sojourn. He thought it would be awkward to be walking in the hotel lobby with such an appearance. He scrubbed his face, combed, came out to lobby and then quickly to the elevators.

His room was open and a hotel supervisor stood in his room looking around, particularly his suitcase. "Yes?" He asked.

"Sorry, sir!" Answered the supervisor, the room service staff had reported that the room looked unused for two days, so I had been asked to check the room. With the security on high alert these days, we are not supposed to take any chances. I am sorry for entering your room without your permission."

Rocky laughed. "No, no! Nothing to worry! Actually some of my friends had suddenly made a program of trekking so we went out to Almora for a couple of days. I was not prepared for this at all! Just see what is the condition of my clothes now!"

"Yes, sir!" he answered, "you do look very tired. May I send you some drink or tea or any other thing you may like?

"Yeah! That sounds like a good idea!" He complimented, "Please send a large blue label on the rocks and some chicken tikka. And please make it very very very fast! If you delay, you might find me snoring and sure won't wake up until tomorrow morning!"

"Sure, sir! In a jiffy!" he smiled and left the room.

Rocky quickly took out the band from his pocket, kept it in the locker in the cupboard, locked it, got rid of his dirty stinking clothes, threw them on the floor and moved to the bath tub.

12

Ankit returned quite late to his new home. A decent two bedroom furnished apartment, which he got possession of without making any efforts what so ever! Just listening to his inner voice. And he also got money. Plenty of it. He always knew something big had been waiting for him. He was not meant for small mundane things. And suddenly he had become rich. So rich, that he could not count his own money! There was no need to count. The inner voice had told him that money will keep getting replenished! He had today, in just one night spent over three thousand bucks. He only wished that the beautiful Romanian girl he met during the day could see him splashing money like this. She would certainly abandon her boy friend and come to him.

Anyway. Once you have money, you will splash and the girls would come like bees come to honey.

He had taken a little too many drinks and was not able to stay awake for long. He did not bother to remove his jeans or jacket and slipped into the bed. Next day he would also buy new jeans and jackets. Today his first priority had been to satisfy his hunger – he had not eaten good food for months together. He recalled the hopeless chicken masala and naans at the shabby stinking restaurant yesterday. Well, that was yesterday!

He did not know when he fell asleep and how long he slept. But something woke him up. It was still pitch dark.

There was no noise. But a small click. Some one was opening the door. He was scared stiff. Inner voice had warned him enough about the thieves. How correct was this inner voice. He had told him to protect himself. He gave him the revolver and had repeatedly told him to shoot the intruder at the earliest. He must not be left alive. He felt sweat on his forehead. He could also feel his body trembling. But then the words of inner voice gave him strength. And direction. Without moving he slowly reached the revolver under his pillow. Caught it correctly with the finger on the trigger. But he did not want to rush things. Probably there was no thief. Probably he may go without harming him. But then he heard the main door open slowly. And some one entering very softly. From his bed he could see only part of the living room. He could see that there was a thin beam of light from a pen torch, which the intruder was moving all round to see whether any one was there or probably to see where the money was.

Ankit kept watching the movement of the light beam. He was hoping that after completing his survey in the living room the thief will go away. But the thief moved towards his room. His grip on the revolver tightened. His trembling trebled. He was full of sweat and could scream any time. And then the light beam fell on his bed. The intruder screamed and turned to run away, but this startled Ankit even more. He directed his pistol towards him and shot. The thief screamed again and fell down. In Ankit's mind the words of his inner voice were echoing… shoot……. shoot…… shoot……. Shoot till all the bullets are fired. The thief must not stay alive.

Falling of the thief and the noise of gunshots had unnerved Ankit. He could not stay back any longer in this room – with a dead man. He ran out of the door, down the stairs and on to the street and kept running. He did not know where he was headed. He just wanted to get away from the dead body lying in his apartment. He wanted to get back to safety. He wanted to get back to his mother. She was the only one who could come to his rescue in this hour of distress. She was the only one who could give him comfort. How safe he would be with his head immersed in her lap. But it was impossible to reach her. She was hundreds of miles away, and he had abandoned this loving mother. He kept running like a possessed man until he hit something and fell. It looked like a large bag lying on the side of the road. But hit by him, the bag moved, and then sat up.

"What is this? Who are you?" Demanded the man who was sleeping on the road side.

Ankit was panting badly and was full of sweat in the cold January morning. But he did not want to get into any argument now. He had to run. He had to run to safety. He tried to get up again when the man saw his gun and caught hold of his hand.

"Hey this gun. Are you running after committing a murder?" shouted the man.

"No, no!" Ankit tried to get his hand free and run leaving the gun there. But the man's grip was strong. He did not leave him. He got up. And began pulling Ankit with him. Ankit had no idea who this man was and what he intended to do with him or where he was taking him to. But he also did not know what to do. He was not used to facing any problems. He was good at running away from them. But now the option of running away also seemed to have run away. He was in a strong tight grip and was being forced to go to some place. As usual, Ankit resigned to his fate.

13

It was not unusual for Pandit to keep drinking till late in the evening and then fall anywhere on the road. And once fallen, he made no efforts to get up. He would rather spend the night there only. Cold or rain did not come in his way, for he was usually covered in his thick police coat which protected him. Usually in the early morning hours he would wake up and orient himself with his location. Then he would walk to his home. He did not get any sermons from his wife or daughter in law, because they had now realized very well that there was no point in repeating those sermons. They had no effect on him. He did not give any part of his salary to them – all of it was spent on his liquor. But still he had a lot of value. Because of his job they had a place to live – almost free. Medical expenses of entire family were taken care by the Government and after he retired, they would continue to get some pension. Even if he died before retiring, the family would get some good compensation. So instead of getting into some argument and losing peace for everyone, they had learnt to live with their predicament. When he asked for food, some food was given to him. When he did not return or did not eat, no one cared. If the coat got wet, his daughter in law would leave it out in the sun and hand him over the other coat. Surprisingly he rarely fell ill due to his adventurous nights out in the cold. So he was really no longer a nuisance for his family. He was just a non entity.

Same situation was at work. Everyone at the police station had accepted the fact that he was good for nothing. In the mornings, though he was still not sober, he had enough sense to come to the police station and sign his attendance register. No work was ever entrusted to him, but all the works which no one wanted to do, were given to him, for there was no need to really work on them, just the formalities had to be completed. He was generally punctual when coming to report for duty, but after an hour or so was difficult to trace. But he did no harm to anyone and people had accepted him as a useless and irrelevant but unavoidable existence.

Today when he reached the police station, the day was about to break. The sky had become slightly bluish. During winters the mornings are late and soon it will be time for shift change. The nightshift personnel were getting ready to start packing up and returning to their homes. Seeing Pandit coming at this hour was an unexpected phenomenon. The In charge of night shift commented, "Why Pandit, had too little in the night so starting early?"

Pandit very proudly produced his catch, "No I caught a murderer. Red handed. You all always underestimate me. But I am the only one to have a caught a murderer red handed and that too so fast."

Ankit was in terrible shape. Tears had started rolling down his eyes. "No sir, I did not kill. He had come to kill me. I was only protecting myself. Please leave me. I will go home."

He did not look like a criminal but more like a school boy caught doing some mischief. No one in the police station could understand anything. The In-charge asked him to sit down opposite him. Even though Ankit had already inadvertently admitted to having done something, he found it difficult to start acting in any direction particularly when the suspect had been brought by Pandit. May be Pandit had a few drinks too many and was harassing this young man. The man could not be a murderer.

Ankit was crying aloud now. What he was saying was incomprehensible. In-charge decided to let him cool down a bit. He sat silently watching him. Everyone in the police station was watching them. In-charge asked Pandit, "Where did you find him? What was he doing?"

"He killed a man and was trying to run away. I chased him and caught." He suddenly recollected about the gun and added, "I then fought with him and snatched his gun." He took the gun out of his pocket and put it on the table.

The sight of gun made everyone think that the matter was not really a pun being played by Pandit as they had been apprehending. It was a much more serious matter.

The In-charge took the gun and inspected it. It was an imported good quality gun. He looked at the man again. It was still difficult to believe that this man possessed this gun. It could be with some rich businessman. The man was not rich. He was a middle class college pass out or a drop out, who could be caught for eve-teasing or brawls on the streets, but could not be expected to be owning licensed revolvers.

"Is this yours?" He asked Ankit.

"No, sir!" he said.

"He is lying, sir!" Shouted Pandit, "I caught him with the gun."

"Where did you get it from?" In-charge addressed Ankit.

"Sir, it was lying in the home."

"In your home? Who else lives with you in your home?"

Ankit pondered over the question for a moment. He recollected the words of his inner voice. It had said several times it was his house. But actually it wasn't. So the answer is yes or no?

"Who else lives with you?" repeated the In-charge.

"No one, sir!" This question was an easier one.

"Whom did you kill?" Asked In-charge.

"No, sir! I did not kill him." He began crying loudly again.

In-charge suddenly realized that it would be better to quickly visit the spot of crime. Once a crowd gathered there, valuable evidence could be lost.

"Where did the incident happen?" He asked Pandit.

Pandit was caught on the wrong foot. He had no idea where the incident took place.

"Ask him." He said. "He should take us to the site."

In-charge looked intently at Pandit. It was difficult to guess what exactly had happened and what had been the role of Pandit in this. Pandit, as usual, could not be relied upon.

He asked his constables to check thoroughly the suspect, make a punch list of all his belongings, then handcuff him and seat in the back of the jeep. The man had three hundred sixty five rupees and a receipt of a restaurant at Connaught Place. Nothing else. No identity, no mobile, no credit cards.

He was handcuffed and seated on the backside of the police jeep where two more constables joined him. He was asked to give directions to the scene of crime.

Pandit was not asked to join the team. Neither did he want to. Morning shift people had started arriving. His longing for the first shot of the day was rising and he was now finding it difficult to continue any further at the police station. Unfortunately, the shop won't be open for another couple of hours. He could try some of his regular companions.

But they too, like him, were difficult to find, and in any case none of them could be expected to be having any liquor left!

The door of the apartment was still slightly ajar. The police team entered and found a man lying on the ground crying in pain. Looking at the police he began pleading loudly, "Save me, save me sir. He will kill me. Take me away sir, please quickly take me away. He may be still around. He will kill me."

The bullet had hit him in the hip and he was unable to get up. But there were no other injuries. The In-charge instructed his constable to get the ambulance and looked around inside the apartment. Some bullets had hit the walls. Except for the pain and inability to move because of the bullet in the hip, and trauma, the victim appeared to be in fairly good shape.

He asked him, "Who shot at you? Who will kill you?"

"Edny. Edny Arem sir! He has already killed my friend and he will kill me now. Take me away soon. Don't wait for ambulance. I will go in the jeep. But take me away immediately, sir!"

In-Charge took out his mobile and made a call. As soon as the response came, he blurted, "Shiv Prasad, sir? You may like to meet Edny Arem. We have him arrested. He is in our lock up now."

He disconnected. Instructed the constables to seal the apartment after the victim was taken out and then to report back at the police station.

14

Rocky had a good night's sleep. In fact more than a night! He had hit the bed before nine and was still in it till 11 in the morning. If the hard day did not lie ahead, he would have continued even longer. But he had a lot of things to do. The meeting was scheduled for evening tomorrow. About three hundred miles north of Rome. All flights to Europe leave late in the night or rather very early morning, reaching the destination in the early hours of morning. Then he would have to travel to the small coastal town and deliver the consignment. Simple job.

Easier said than done. After a long time – several months he was having to do it himself. All these days his assistants had been handling these small delivery jobs. Now Bhure was out of circulation. He wondered whether Bhure had returned to the apartment and whether Ankit had killed him. There was no way to know. Probably he should have left a phone with Ankit too. But then immediately patted himself for not having done so. Ankit would likely be arrested soon and naturally, with the phone. So why to get such an exposure? He had no time to go back and confirm also. But he believed that Bhure won't come back so soon. He would probably wait for a few more days before returning. The bigger fear was that if Bhure returned and Ankit wasn't there, then he would easily get away. And may never be caught.

He did not have the wherewithal to follow up on him or keep track of his family. He had kept his organization very lean and had organized it very well. Most of the people did not know each other and were not required to contact them. He passed on very specific instructions as and when required. And the men carried out those instructions to the letter. Bigger organisation meant bigger risks. At least some very trusted lieutenants should be there at key positions to keep lower level operating employees under continuous supervision and control. He had so far not found any one who could be trusted. Not even his girl friend.

Under the circumstances, all that he could do was to leave certain things to fate. He hoped that Ankit would not develop cold feet when he encounters Bhure. Anyway, presently he did not want to waste his time on these unwelcome thoughts. The need of the hour was action.

He switched on his laptop and began searching for the flights going to Rome. His preference was direct flights. Direct flights are always safer. Only two airports to cross. Only Alitalia and Air India flew directly to Rome and then realized that Air India shared the code with Alitalia. Bhure Lal would have been taking this flight only. So there was no need to send any messages for a change in schedule. He was in good luck as at least thirty percent of the seats were vacant. About the return journey he would decide on the actual day of travel. He switched off the laptop.

He turned to his bag. Opened it and took out five mobile phones. One was of Pratap's. He threw it back in the suitcase. Checked the numbers carved on the back side of the body and then took one of them, switched it on and waited for the signals to show. As the phone started getting signal, he opened the contact list and pressed the only number appearing on it. The response was quite quick.

"When do we meet?" He asked.

"Two hours from now. Nehru Park." The crisp, to the point answer. No other conversation.

He disconnected, switched off the phone and threw it back in the suitcase.

He had two hours now. Going back to Geeta Colony would be possible if he used his own car. Or may be a hired taxi? But again that carried a risk of getting a relationship established. He was a very safe player. He had long innings to play and did not want to risk getting caught attempting a quick six or four. Careful, small steps would go a long way, he concluded.

He locked up his suitcase and was about to move out when suddenly recalled something and once again picked out the mobile phones from his suitcase. Checked the numbers on the back again, and then took out one, switched on and called a number from it.

As soon as the other side responded, he whispered, "Billu, send five in a car, park the car at Nehru Park and hand me the keys at Hotel Ashok. Quick."

Relaxed a bit, he moved out to enjoy a leisurely swim in the pool. Once at the pool, he realized that the pool was not heated. Though the day was warm, water would be quite cold. Getting into the pool wouldn't be a great idea. No one was swimming. There were some sunbathing on the pool chairs. He just looked around and walked back to his room, changed, and walked out again. Walking up to the reception, he asked for a vehicle to drop him at Hotel Ashok. He would come back on his own later, he said.

He went into the lobby of Hotel Ashok and began walking in the shopping arcade. Bought a pack of India Kings and a lighter and dashed into some old acquaintance. Shook hands with him and exchanged pleasantries. After some time with the same leisurely pace walked out of the hotel and towards Nehru Park. He looked around himself. No one seemed to be following him. He checked the keys of the car his acquaintance had handed him inconspicuously at the cigarette shop. He went into the park and continued to a corner where a bench lay behind some bushes. An ideal rendezvous for the first date!

He sat down on the bench, lit a cigarette and looked at his watch. A man was walking towards him from the other side of the park. Coming closer, he asked whether he had a light. He took out the lighter and passed on.

"Edny?" The stranger asked.

"Edny Arem" Rocky answered.

The man handed him a packet. He took it, handed him the keys of the car and looked around. Park was quite deserted. Some people enjoying the sun were a little away. No one seemed to be interested in them. He walked out of the park on the Yashwant Place side and got into the nearest taxi.

He got down at RK Puram sector 6, walked for some distance and entered into a flat. He stayed there for about half an hour and then came out again with a jacket neatly folded in a plastic cover after dry cleaning. He hailed a taxi and asked him to take him to hotel Le Meridien.

At the hotel, he handed over the jacket for screening by their X-ray machine and walked past the door frame metal detector. Once inside, he picked up the jacket again, took the elevator and walked back to his room.

Couple of hours later, he picked up his bags and walked out again, went to the cashier and checked out of the hotel. At the porch he handed over his card to the valet for bringing back his car. A couple of minutes later he was driving to his home at Golf Links.

Shailaja opened the door and hugged him. "You know how many days you have been away? You had promised to return in two days and it is five days now." She complained.

"Yes, I know darling!" he kissed her as they walked inside the house, "You know my job is such. You never know how long it will take. Unfortunately, I have to leave again in a couple of hours."

"What? No way! Please slow down, Rocky! You are spoiling your health. No work is so important. Rest for at least a day and then go."

"Well," he tried to console her, "this time I guess I will not delay like this. I should be back in four days."

"Four days? Where are you going?"

Rocky smiled, "Again? Such questions cannot be answered, darling!"

Shailaja was fully aware that Rocky was involved in some kind of illegal activities. But she hardly cared. She knew the value of money and it really did not matter how it came. Rocky seemed to have the potential. In spite of his humble background he had maintained high profile friends, lived a lavish life and now was on to something big. Until graduation, he lived practically off his friends, but soon after graduation, he began transforming. His average middle class wardrobe was replaced by high class designer clothes, and soon he was throwing his own lavish parties. Shailaja had so far been ignoring his advances, but now she began taking him more seriously. It was quite easy to win him over – he was anyway falling head over heels for her. It won't be long before she would have complete control of Rocky, the business he had got into and his wealth.

"See, we have so little time, why don't we make best use of it?" Said Rocky with a naughty twinkle in his eyes, pulling Shailaja closer to himself. He put his arm around her waist to pull her even closer and placed his lips on hers. Shailaja closed her eyes. His right hand moved up on her side and lightly brushed against her breast. Her whole body shivered. Even after having lived together for about an year, her body responded so ecstatically to his touches, pleased him no ends. He almost instantaneously warmed up to her reaction and the pressure on her lips increased. From her lips he began sliding down slowly side ways to her cheeks, ears, neck and further down along the neckline of her blouse. Her body stiffened and breathing quickened. He buried his head between her breasts. They both lost all sense of time and place and remained entangled on the sofa till late in the evening when Rocky suddenly began picking his clothes and said, "I am getting late. Would you please drop me at the airport?"

"Of course. But you haven't packed your bags."

"Don't worry! I will buy everything afresh there!" Smiled Rocky.

Shailaja did not quite like it. She looked straight into his eyes, and said, "You know such things stink of…."

"Infidelity!" Rocky completed the sentence with a smile. Then added, "Shaila, I have nothing to prove my integrity. But if you can take my word for it, please do. I am not going to any other girlfriend, but for some work related to my business. And I will be off communication for the next four days. I hope things will improve soon and I will not have to travel like this. Can you bear with me till then?"

Shailaja nodded, still not fully convinced.

An hour later Shailaja dropped him at the airport. He turned round the car towards the driving seat, pushed his face inside the window and kissed her a good bye, repeating, "Please believe me, I am not cheating on you!" Shailaja did not really care, but at the same time she did not want a competitor for her target.

He stood outside, waived, and waited for her to drive away. As she moved, he walked towards the monitor near the entry to the terminal, looking for his flight. Check in was in progress. The flight was to take off in another hour from gate number 23, so check in would close soon. But he did not hurry towards the gate. Instead, he walked towards the washrooms at the end of the terminal building. Walked in, looked around and moved towards the farthest WC. No one stood near that and from this end of the washroom, it remained slightly out of sight.

He entered, closed the door with some noise, but did not bolt it. The door slowly got half opened again. Rocky kept on standing there for some time. Then took the wrist band out of his pocket and wore it on his left wrist. He still kept waiting in the WC for a few minutes and then started out again.

At the main entry to the terminal, two security personnel were checking the tickets and identity of the passengers. He stood on a side waiting for the queue to end and as soon as it ended, he just walked in, then past the check-in counters and to the security hold area.

Being late in the evening, there were no domestic flights and one part of the security hold area was deserted. A couple of security officers sat on chairs, certainly not very alert as no passengers were allowed in this side. Rocky walked to this part. The lights on the door frame metal detectors were blinking indicating that they were still switched on even though no one expected to pass through them. He went round one the frames past the snoozing security guard and into the waiting lounge area.

The monitor showed that boarding had started in Alitalia flight through gate number 23. He walked to gate number 23 and once again waited for the queue to end. As the last of the sleep weary passenger showed his boarding pass to the security guard and moved on, Rocky followed him with a very narrow gap into the aircraft.

Standing at the beginning of the Business class seats he took stock of the available vacant seats. Travelling in business class was easier and safer. There were two seats vacant. One was in the first row, next to some senior business executive. Sitting here would be okay except whenever service was going on, because the hostess would come halfway through this seat to serve this man. He decided to take the other one, next to a European girl. It would have been the best possible seat for him, as this was in the middle row. Both seats had access to aisle so the girl would not have to disturb him. But as he moved towards this seat, the girl threw her blanket, cushions and a thick book on this vacant seat. Rocky stopped. Sitting next to this girl may not be as safe as he had thought.

He was about to move on to the economy section but stopped again. Most of the passengers were seated but in between some one would get up to open the bin above the seat and the hostesses also kept moving. The aisle must be free and must remain free until he reached his chosen seat.

It was safer to wait standing in this corner of business class section where space was more and movements fewer.

The doors closed and announcements began. This was a good time to move. He quickly moved along the aisle taking stock of the vacant seats. Quite a few were vacant but he was looking for a seat from his own point of view. Finally in the twenty eighth row he saw a fat old lady sitting alone. She would normally not care to move to the window seat. He thought. She would also not move much. But he must get access to the window seat past her. He looked around again. Though many seats were vacant, passengers had occupied the aisle and window seats leaving the middle ones empty. It was not possible for Rocky to occupy a middle seat without disturbing the passenger on the aisle seat.

Should he return and try his luck in the vacant business class seat? Now the welcome drink must have been served and the hostess may not disturb until the flight was stable in the sky and seat belt signs were switched off. He rushed back to the first row. The executive was immersed in the news paper. The used wet towel was lying on the arms rest and so was half empty glass of champagne. He sat down on the vacant seat. The executive probably got a feel of someone coming there and turned to look but finding no one, returned to his newspaper.

The hostess came back to pick up the towel and the glass. He held his breath, pulled in his legs as close to the seat as possible and his body pushed hard against the seat. The hostess returned and he relaxed again.

The doors were closed and aerobridge retreated. The plane began moving backwards slowly and with this the hostess came back with the demo kit. She unfolded the table tray from the arm rest and kept the safety jacket and the oxygen mask on it and began demonstrating the use of safety belt. The few minutes seemed like a few months to Rocky. He again held back his breath and kept praying that she does not keep anything on the seat. Luckily, she didn't. Rocky again heaved a sigh of relief after she left.

The plane took off and was still rising at a steep angle when Rocky got up and moved backwards. He did not want to take any risk of a suspicion arising. He stood at the back of the plane waiting and working out his strategy. The steep angle was making it difficult for him to stand. He leaned against the toilet door, intently watching the passengers on the aisle seats. None of them appeared to be eagerly waiting for the seatbelt signs to switch off. The plane became level and the Captain switched off the seat belt sign. The hostesses began their movements. Rocky was relaxed to see the fatso also making a move to come out of her seat. As soon as she got up, Rocky rushed in and occupied the window seat. Now he could happily sleep rest of the night!

Suddenly another fear struck him. All three seats being empty, the fatso might lift the armrests between the seats and fall flat using all the three seats after a few minutes. How to stop her? His fertile mind got the solution in a flash. He took the bottle of water from the seat pocket, and emptied it on the middle seat.

The lady returned to her seat, and as he had feared, began lifting the center arm rests. Just then she saw the wet seat and cursed. Pressed the button to call the hostess. But the hostess could offer her no solution. She was shocked to find the seat wet, but could not get a clue on how it could have got wet. She instead thought that the lady herself had dropped an open bottle of water on this seat. Finally she left saying that the seat could not be dried so soon. It was vacant anyway so she must not be bothered. The lady was unhappy, but had no options. She reclined her seat and began dozing off again.

Meal service began. The delicious aroma of food reminded Rocky that he had not taken a meal in the night. In fact he had not had a decent meal for four days in a row. While on the lookout for Bhure lal, he used to just pick up crumbs from here and there. Yesterday, after returning from Geeta colony, he was so tired that after a shower and a double peg of blue label, he had fallen asleep. Today morning he got up late and then rushed to complete the half done business after a quick bite. He had planned to have a good meal at home but Shailaja's inviting body didn't leave him any time for food. Now he needed something to eat.

The hostess came and asked the old lady. She was sleeping, but got up. She asked for Indian selection and was served a tray with chicken curry, a couple of paranthas and rice. She unrolled the aluminium foil to take out the paranthas and began taking out the plastic cutlery from the small cellophane packet.

Rocky could not resist the temptation. He stealthily pulled out a piece of parantha from the aluminium foil. The lady was busy pulling out cutlery. She could not notice. Rocky wanted a piece of chicken also and kept gazing at the woman to find the opportune moment. She uncovered all the cellophane and aluminium foil covered plastic bowls to expose raita, dal, chicken curry, salad and some dessert. Then she picked up a piece of cucumber with her fork, put it in her mouth and turned to look at the table of the other passenger sitting across the aisle.

Rocky did not lose a moment. He carefully picked up the piece of chicken, rolled it in his parantha and began eating. The lady turned her eyes to her tray and found something amiss. She looked startled and even looked on her lap and sideways, under the seats to find where her piece of chicken had gone. She could not find it. She could not even make up her mind on what to do. If she asks the hostess, then, what should she ask? Where has my chicken gone? Well madam, you must have eaten it! If you need another piece, please let me know – don't beat around the bush!

Rocky was enjoying her predicament. He had eaten the parantha quickly, and though very hungry, he did not really like it. Now he kept watching the lady eating her dinner but every now and then looking around, inside the tray, on the table and on the next seat to find the missing piece of chicken. The fun show ended finally and the woman relapsed into her nap again. The hostess cleared the table. Soon the lights were off and the entire plane looked like a large community bedroom. There were a couple of die hards who continued to watch their TVs. In the dark cabin, the flickering lights of their TV monitors did disturb somewhat. But Rocky too fell asleep soon. His long sleep at the Meridienne had not fully made up for the lost sleep.

He woke up after a few hours and this time with another pressing need. He had to go to the loo. The lady was sleeping soundly, snoring lightly. Rocky stood up and looked around. The seats behind and ahead were full. So there was no possibility of jumping across the back rest. There was no option, but to disturb this sleeping monolith.

He finally took the wrist band out of his wrist and tapped the lady. She got up, and cursing inaudibly, turned sideways to make way for him. Rocky quickly relieved himself, and then went onwards to the trolley parked near the pantry. There were some sandwiches, cakes, chocolates, wines, beer and other drinks. He picked up a can of beer and a couple of sandwiches and walked back to his seat. Tapped the old lady and went in to enjoy the sandwiches and beer in the dark solitude of his window seat. He reclined the seat, finished the beer and sandwiches, slipped on his wrist band and began dozing.

Couple of hours later the frenzy began. The lights were switched on and the hostesses began serving breakfast and tea. The old lady got up and looked to her right where someone had got in to sleep during the night. She could not find any one and looked perplexed. Rocky laughed without making a noise. From now on the lady would start believing that she was getting old! She took some tea and began sipping, turning her head to her right from time to time to confirm that it was indeed vacant, and either the person who was sleeping here in the night had gone out somehow without disturbing her, or she had been dreaming. What did she finally conclude would be very interesting! Thought Rocky.

The flight was now preparing to land. Outside was still dark. Dawn would break only after they had landed. He began developing strategy for disembarking. Probably it would be best to continue sitting until most had disembarked.

The plane landed and soon the entire sleeping gentry was on its feet. He always wondered why after having waited long hours, the passengers can't demonstrate patience for a couple of minutes more and make the exit look a little more civilized. The phenomena is always the same all over the world, across all airlines, be it a domestic 40 minute long or an international thirteen hour flight!

The passengers began disembarking. Rocky got up and began following the last of the passengers keeping a respectable distance from him. Some passengers with children or who needed support, kept sitting, waiting for the aisle to get cleared of the crowd and supporting crew to arrive.

The whole crowd was moving towards the immigration desks. Rocky evaluated his options. The counter for diplomats had just one passenger waiting while one was at the counter. He walked past the waiting passenger and waited silently behind the one standing on the counter. Then as he moved, he too quickly moved out of the immigration enclosure.

The crowd had gathered near the conveyor belts. He had nothing to collect. He had no cabin bag either. But he was very alert and looked around carefully. And suddenly stiffened. An official with a sniffer dog was moving around the bags. The dog would also sniff at some of the passengers. Moving further was very dangerous. The reverence his camouflage had been attracting from the humans may probably not be extended by the canine. His movement must be surreptitious and swift, before the canine notices him and gets interested.

He looked around, and began walking in the opposite direction round the conveyor belts. And then kept on walking through the customs green channel, keeping safe distances from any other passengers. He was soon out of the airport terminal. But the danger still lurked. At the airport the authorities are generally more vigilant than at other places. Any wrong move may ruin the entire game.

He began walking towards the parking lot. It was a good kilometer walk by the time he reached a public toilet. He looked around and found no one. He looked up and found a CCTV camera. There was no escape from this, he thought. But would any body be really watching a deserted parking lot? The footage may be watched later if something happens here. Since no one was in the vicinity, the chances of something happening within a short time frame appeared remote.

He fished out some coins from his pocket, slid a euro in the slot and moved in. Inside, he again removed his wrist band, looked at himself in the mirror, washed his face, combed and straightened his jacket. The Jacket which had been so uncomfortable in Delhi and in the plane, had suddenly become the most comfortable and useful piece of his dress in the freezing temperatures of Rome.

He walked out of the toilet and walked towards one of the cars parked there. Took out his mobile, switched on and dialed the already stored number.

"Mr Burre?" An Italian accent.

"Yes. Where do we meet?" Rocky asked.

"You sound different." Crackled the other side.

Rocky appreciated the sharp instinct of the respondent.

He said, "You are right, Peiro. Mr. Bhure could not come. I am Edny. Edny Arem."

"Oh! So good to have you again, Edny! I am sorry, I did not bring a buick. You will have to travel in a smaller car! Please walk to parking lot number twenty six. I will pick you there."

"Never mind about the car, Peiro! I am walking to parking lot twenty six."

Parking lot was about another half a kilometer walk. The sun had risen a little higher and promised a bright and warm day ahead. As he approached the parking lot, head lights of a black medium sized car lit up and were off again. He began walking towards it. The car pulled out of the parking bay and stopped near him. He opened the door and got in. The car sped away.

"How is the day scheduled, Peiro?"

"Well, you may check in to the hotel Barcelo for a few hours, get fresh and in the mean time I may get a better car for you and then we shall drive down to Piombino. From there we shall go to Caro in a beautiful yacht. Mr. Luigi would be so glad to meet you." Peiro said, "Why did you not inform that Burre was not coming and you were coming instead?"

"Bhure Lal ran into some problem last night. I had no one in a ready position to move, so came myself. It was all too sudden and very hectic."

"When do you plan to return?"

"Tomorrow morning. I might take the same flight back home, but before that I will have to check the seats position."

"Tomorrow morning makes it very tight. But we shall try!" Peiro said, driving in to the porch of hotel Barcelo.

"Here are the keys of your room. You are checked in by the name Stefano. If any one asks, pretend you don't understand. Only tell 'Stefano, friend, coming!' Be ready to move at about three pm, after your lunch."

Rocky walked into the room. It was an average hotel room, fit for Bhure lal. Rocky used to stay in such hotels about an year ago. Now except for situations like the present one, he stayed in large wonderfully furnished luxury suites. He took out his wrist band and put it in the locker, hung his jacket carefully in the wardrobe and then undressed completely; throwing away all the clothes he had been wearing, carelessly. He jumped into the bath and came out after about forty minutes, looking very fresh. He ordered some breakfast over the intercom, wrapped himself in the bathrobe, switched on the TV and sat down on the sofa waiting for the breakfast. After the breakfast, he put the tray out in the corridor, switched on 'do not disturb" sign and slipped into the bed.

15

Shiv Prasad drove recklessly. It was difficult for him to believe that Geeta Colony Police station had arrested Edny Arem so fast. In his opinion, this was one of the most inefficient police stations in the capital, manned by lazy, corrupt alcoholics devoid of common sense even. In fact he intended to visit the police station today afternoon to enquire into the progress made in the search of the place where this Pratap lived. Elizabeth sitting on his side had no different views. But now she was worrying more about the driving of Shiv Prasad. The morning office goers had already crowded the streets with their cars and two wheelers and impatiently drove into every small gap appearing between two cars in between two lanes. In fact the lanes had lost their meaning. Cars moved as haphazardly as they could. No one seemed to be following any road discipline, but tempers were lost and expletives took over as soon as someone else drove in front of another car, cutting lane and block their narrow stretch of road ahead. Road rage was terribly common on Delhi Roads, and more often than not ended in to shootings and killings.

The Police car of Shiv Prasad had no edge over others, except that he was given a go signal by the constable on duty at manned crossings. But there were hardly any manned crossings. Other cars gave him a nasty look when he tried to cut into their path, without giving a thought to the urgency that he might be facing. But the good part was that no one could gather enough courage to come out and affront him because of the police car and his uniform.

It took him almost an hour to reach the Geeta Colony police station. He was immediately brought to the lock up where a fragile looking young man in his early twenties stood with his usual forlorn and frightened look. Just one look and Shiv Prasad could tell that as he had feared, these people were wasting his time.

He looked at the SHO and frowned, "He is Edny Arem?"

"Yes, sir!" The SHO answered without any confidence or concern, "He tried to kill another person here early in the morning and was running away when we nabbed him. The victim told that he was Edny Arem."

"Sir, I am not Edny Arem. I did not try to kill any one. It was a mistake. Sir, please leave me." The accused began crying loudly.

"OK. First let me talk to the cop who caught him." Said Shiv Prasad, "Where is he?"

"Sir, he was on the night duty. He has gone home now." SHO answered. He was afraid that if Shiv Prasad met Pandit, things might take a different turn.

"Is the victim alive?"

"Yes, sir! He is in the Government hospital. Said to be out of danger."

"I would have liked to see him first." Said Shiv Prasad, "but since we are here, let's have a small chit chat with this guy. Bring him in to the office."

They all sat in the SHO's office. The suspect was brought in. He continued crying of his innocence.

Shiv Prasad looked at his face and once again was convinced without asking a single question that this man was not the culprit, but had run into trouble out of stupidity.

Nevertheless, without making his thoughts open, in his gruff police tone, he asked, "What is your name?"

"Ankit, sir! Ankit Arora."

"What do you do?"

"Sir, I am looking for a job. I have passed Hotel Management." He spoke good chaste English, as is usually spoken by high class hotel staff.

"Where do you live?"

"Sir, my parents live in Panchkula near Chandigarh. I was studying in Trivandrum. Now after completing my studies, I came to Delhi to find a job."

"Where do you live in Delhi?" His voice seemed to be more stern.

"No where sir." He was stammering. I lived with the employees of Dahiya Lunch home for one night and …." There was something which he was finding difficult to divulge.

"You did not live in the house where this happened?"

"No, sir!" His mouth had dried up. "I came there only last night."

"How did you come there? Who brought you there?"

He thought for a while and then said "Sir, my inner voice." He swallowed, "It guided me all the way to this flat and showed me where the key was. And it said that this house was mine.

"But sir, prior to this I had never seen this house. I don't know whose house is it. I am innocent sir!" he started crying again.

"Stop this crap, and stop crying immediately." Thundered Shiv Prasad, "You understand the meaning of third degree, don't you?"

Ankit's already white face seemed to have drained off the last drop of blood. Shiv Kumar's gaze was penetrating him like an x-ray.

"Why did you kill him?"

"Sir, my inner voice told me several times to shoot when a thief burgles into my house. This man was thief sir. He wanted to kill me. He came in very late in the night when I was sleeping. My inner voice had told me that if I did not kill him, he would kill me." Ankit was trembling.

Though his narrative could at best be derided, Shiv Prasad was still of the opinion that this man has been set up. He was stupid, if not insane. And someone had taken advantage of his stupidity. May be he was hypnotized to carry out this killing and may be to commit some more crimes in the future. But one thing that he was sure of, was that questioning this guy won't lead him anywhere.

He put his last question, "who is Edny Arem?"

"Edny Arem?" His ignorance appeared genuine, "I don't know any one by that name, sir!"

Shiv Prasad asked the SHO to lock him up again.

Shiv Prasad, Elizabeth, SHO and another constable left for the Government Hospital.

The victim was in a small cabin with a constable guard on duty outside. Seeing them he stood up and saluted. The victim was asleep. He had been given some sedatives. Shiv Prasad asked the constable on duty to call the doctor or the nurse handling this case. In a couple of minutes the doctor came.

"Sir, this was not a serious injury. A Bullet had hit him in the upper thigh. That has been removed. Nothing much to worry about. But the victim is in trauma. He is hysterical and keeps shouting that someone will come and kill him.

So we have given him some tranquilizers. He should be in a position to give a statement in about an hour."

"Can we not reduce the one hour to a few minutes?" smiled Shiv Prasad.

"I recommend not, sir!" The doctor said in an uncompromising tone, "He may break into hysteria again, and won't be able to give any meaningful statement."

"By the way, could you find the identity of this person?" Shiv Prasad asked.

"Not really, sir! Only that his name is Bhure Lal, and he lived in the apartment where the attempt on his life was made."

"Then let's go have a look at the site of crime." Shiv Prasad turned to the SHO, "I hope no one has disturbed the place and it is sealed off properly."

"Of course, sir!" Answered SHO, "it was an apartment. The apartment has been sealed."

They all reached the apartment. It was all quiet. Few bystanders stood outside narrating the events of last night and the morning to new comers. As they proceeded to open the lock, these people closed in and were shooed away by the constable.

They walked in and closed the door to avoid disturbance. The SHO showed the place where victim was found. The room was clean and nicely furnished. The floor had splattered blood marks. The walls on one side had some bullet marks. Apparently the bullets had rained in from the bedroom which was adjacent to the living room. Shiv Prasad moved to the bedroom. The bed was crumpled. Apparently the attacker had been on the bed and fired upon this man as he entered or as he was trying to run away. There were no signs of a skirmish or resistance. Every thing in the bed room appeared to be in place. He opened the drawer on the side table. There were a few CDs, a pen and other sundry items. Nothing of consequence. The man living here led an easy life, but nothing pointed towards his occupation or interests. He opened the cupboard and was shocked. There lied an AK47 assault rifle. He turned to look at the SHO. The SHO and Elizabeth also appeared to be in shock. There were some clothes neatly folded and some hanging, but besides this, there was nothing. There was a large size locker about half the breadth of the cupboard. He pulled it. It was unlocked. Inside was full of currency notes, in rupees five hundred and rupees hundred denomination. He asked Elizabeth to call the team to search the entire apartment carefully. Now he was confident that he was on to something big.

They went back to the hospital. The doctor informed him that the patient could be questioned now, but he was still not in a stable frame of mind.

As Shiv Prasad approached him, he started crying aloud, "sir, save me, save me…. He will kill me. He will come in and kill. He is very dangerous….."

"Don't worry!" Shiv Prasad tried to pacify him, "we have arrested him. He cannot come now."

"How could you have arrested him? He is a ghost!"

"Ghost?" Shocked Shiv Prasad turned to gauge the reaction of Elizabeth and SHO. They had no different reaction.

"Yes, sir! He is invisible." Cried Bhure Lal, "He may be present here also. And he will kill me."

"Who is he? And why would he kill you?" Asked Shiv Prasad.

"I don't know who is he, sir. We know him as Edny Arem only. He is not visible. He only orders. If we don't do it, he will kill. He has already killed Pratap. And now he will kill me."

Shiv Prasad knew that he was not far from his destination, but the mystery was incredible. He recalled the statement of Ankit Arora. He was guided by his "inner voice" to get into this house and to kill the person who entered this house! Indeed it was this Edny Arem! Whosoever he was.

"But why did he kill Pratap?"

"I don't know sir." Bhure Lal said, "He did not carry out the orders of Edny Arem. And probably he was going to inform the police. Now he might be seeing me talking to you and he will kill me."

"What orders he did not carry out?" He asked.

"Sir first take me to a safe place. Don't leave me here. He can come in any time. He is very dangerous. He is every where."

Shiv Prasad thought for a while then asked again, "The house where you were attacked, is yours?"

"No, sir!" he answered, "I and Pratap lived there. It was given to us by Edny Arem."

"How did you get the AK47 there?"

He again looked seriously troubled. Then he decided to tell, "Sir, this gun was brought by Pratap from the border. He was supposed to hand it over to Edny Arem. He did not give it to him. So Edny Arem killed him."

"When and where was he supposed to hand it over to Edny?"

"Sir, on the morning of January 26th, near hotel Meridien." Bhure had now probably overcome the fear of this man and had decided to divulge all secrets. He continued, "Sir, we both discussed till late in the night. We were sure he had very serious terrorist plans. He is invisible. So he could carry the loaded AK47 at the fencing where all VVIPs sit and watch the Republic Day Parade. It would have been very easy for him to kill all the VVIPs and senior Armed forces officers in five minutes flat and he would have run away without being spotted by anyone. The country would have been ruined in five minutes. So we decided not to follow his orders but to inform the police. But he somehow came to know and killed him before he could reach the police station. I have been trying to hide from him since then."

Sweat appeared on the forehead of Shiv Prasad. Such a sinister plan! He shivered. He recalled that at Akbar road police station, no one could see Pratap's killer though an alert constable like Ram Singh had been watching the entire incident from beginning. How could he be invisible? There was certainly something more than what meets the eye. The threat was real. And the brain behind it was free. Not only free, he was beyond the reach of any one. He could do whatever he liked without being seen. The security of the country was so seriously at stake and no one had an inkling. And no one had a clue of who this person was and how he operated and if he had some more accomplices, where were they. He thought ruefully.

From the corner of his eye, he saw the SHO and Elizabeth too were stunned and sweating like him, in this cold January morning.

"How does he give you instructions?" He asked.

"Through small paper slips which tell us to switch on our mobiles phones at a particular time and then he gives instructions over the mobile." He took out a mobile phone from his pocket. With that came out a small paper slip.

He signaled Elizabeth to take both. She took them, read the slip and almost jumped out of her seat, "Sir, please read the name written at the bottom of the slip….. backwards!"

It read 'AIDNI RM"

As if lightening had struck him, stunned Shiv Prasad kept on looking at the slip for some time. The stories he had heard about the sensational case more than two decades ago flashed in his mind. A dangerous terrorist outfit was uncovered by some young ordinary citizen, who had learnt to become invisible. He used his technique to penetrate deep into the outfit and exposed them. In the process he had landed himself into serious risk of his own life and the life of his girlfriend and other family members. But undeterred, he continued and helped the police eliminate this gang. Following this the young man disappeared into oblivion. No one knew his whereabouts. People forgot all about him, but sometimes the old timers in the police department talked about the case. This young man had given himself the nick name Mr. India.

And now history had come back to repeat itself. Mr. India had at that time helped the police to nab the terrorist gang, but this time, he was on the other side. And so perhaps he had reversed his name. Shiv Prasad shivered at the thought of how dreadful this man can become, if not brought under control immediately. He left the questioning, bolted out of the cabin leaving hurried instructions for the SHO to increase security for this patient by five times and keep all doors and windows closed at all times.

16

Octogenarian Srinivasulu was leading a peaceful retired life in a beautiful small bungalow in Gurgaon with his wife. He did not have many visitors and he himself went out only for some special police and Government functions where he was invited from time to time. He had an illustrious past and the glory of his past was enough to get invited to such functions. Newly appointed IPS officers sometimes visited him to seek his blessings. But Shiv Prasad and Elizabeth were neither fresh IPS officers nor had come seeking blessings. Shiv Prasad needed some specific information about a very famous case Srinivasulu had handled during his career and in fact this case had made him famous the world over.

Shiv Prasad came directly to the point, "Sir, is this guy, Mr. India still living, or his children or any of his close friends or associates whom I can meet?"

Srinivasulu remained silent for a long time as if pondering what to say.

Then very carefully balancing his words, he asked, "Why do you need to know?"

"Sir, I have a hunch that this guy has either himself or through some accomplices, got involved in some antinational activities. They are now hatching a very serious and dangerous plan, which I would not like to reveal at this stage, but it is imperative that all these people are caught immediately and put behind bars. I assure you, the danger is far more serious than you may be able to think of."

"To even think that Anil could be involved in such a thing, is blasphemy. I have always considered him at a level equivalent to our revered freedom fighters. But nevertheless, since you are so disturbed, I will introduce you to one of his adopted children. He can tell you about him and may be even arrange your meeting with him." He picked up a pack of visiting cards, took one out and began dialing the number on his mobile.

"Hari," he spoke softly, "Can you come to me quickly? Someone wants to meet you." He disconnected and sat with a grim face.

"I don't know what made you form such an opinion, but thinking such a thing gives me a feeling of guilt. I am sure you will feel the same way when you know more about him."

Both were silent for a while and then he began again, "You have not read how he risked his life to fight against those so powerful terrorists? How simple at heart he was? He is continuing his same simple ways. He would certainly give his life for the country without thinking for a second. He would side with terrorists? Not for the wealth of this whole world! Not for the life of his dearest ones…. No, nothing can deter him….. nothing can overcome his love for his country."

Shiv Prasad noticed, he was crying. He felt sorry and guilty but the facts he knew were something which could not be ignored. It was no coincidence that the man could remain invisible and name himself reverse of Mr India! There had to be a link. And if Anil himself was not involved then also the culprit had to be one from his close contacts. One with whom he had shared this top secret.

Hari came in, touched Srinivasulu's feet and sat down. Srinivasulu's eyes were still moist. He waved towards Shiv Prasad.

"*Beta*, Mr. Shiv Prasad is a very efficient and respected officer in the Crime Branch. He wants to know something about Anil. I was not sure if I should tell him anything. I have only said that he is happily living in some part of this country. Rest I leave to you."

Hari looked at Shiv Prasad, and said, "Sir, my father does not wish to be contacted by any one. He is in a small village leading his own happy life. May I request you not to take the trouble of meeting him?"

Shiv Prasad's suspicion returned. His voice turned slightly business like. "There is a serious issue of national importance. National security is at risk. I must meet him. And meet him at the earliest."

"He lives in a small remote village helping the poor and orphaned children. In fact I am one of the orphans brought up by him. I don't think he will be able to help you, sir!"

"As I said, I must meet him irrespective of whether or not he can be of help."

Hari's voice also became a little terse. "And if I refuse to tell you where he lives?"

"I may have to arrest you."

Hari got up, and raised his hands in front of Shiv Prasad as if offering to put hand cuffs.

Shiv Prasad looked helplessly at Srinivasulu.

"Shiv Prasad," Srinivasulu said, "You have never seen Anil. I have known him very well. The same self esteem, honesty and love for the country has been percolating down to all his children. You will not be able to get anywhere this way. Hari would be of great help if you share the concerns that you have."

Shiv Prasad did not know how to begin. He said, "Look Hari, your father knew some technique to become invisible. And from what I have read about him, he saved the country from some dreaded terrorists. But then he disappeared. This all happened more than twenty five years ago. Now the same technique of becoming invisible is being applied for spreading terrorism in the country. I need to know urgently with whom has your father shared this technique."

He did not say the part that he feared that his father had got tired of that life of deprivation in some obscure village and himself was using this to earn a lot of money. He thought again. If what Bhure lal was saying was even partly correct, this reverse Mr. India might have been promised several million dollars.

Hari smiled. "Certainly, I will take you to him. But please promise that his whereabouts would not be revealed to any one."

"I promise. Unless I have to reveal it in the national interest."

"Of course."

17

Rocky found a complete set of clothes in the cupboard. He put them on, took out the wrist band from the locker and put it in his trouser pocket. Put the jacket on and set out to see Peiro. He was waiting at the portico. As soon as he got in, the shiny silver colored Lamborghini vroomed out. The city took about an hour to pass and then the speedometer never fell below hundred.

Countryside of Italy was beautiful. The roads clean and well maintained. On the road side leafless trees stood testimony to the cold prevailing weather. The road ran almost parallel to the sea shore and up and down the hilly terrain. From time to time they could get a good view of the sea. They were keeping to the highways and there were no stops anywhere. The drive was pleasant. Outside was cold but clear.

Darkness soon enveloped them. By the time they reached Piombino, it was past seven PM. They left the highway and took a narrow road finally reaching a point surrounded by hills on three sides and the fourth side open to the sea. Because of the hills, this site could not be seen from the highway. This was a good site for picnics. There was a small jetty which was probably used for berthing small boats or other water sports.

Peiro rang someone from his mobile. In a few minutes a beautiful yacht came and berthed at the jetty. A man from the boat came out, took the keys of Lamborghini from Peiro and drove it away. Peiro and Rocky got into the boat. It was a lavish boat, equipped with a couple of bed rooms, a lounge complete with bar, dining room and kitchen. They sat down at the bar. Peiro took out a bottle of white wine from the refrigerator and showed it to Rocky, "This is a widely appreciated wine from Bordeau. I guess you will love it."

Rocky looked at the label and nodded. He poured the wine. And they began enjoying the boat trip to Caro. Peiro began narrating the villa Luigi had at Caro. It took them about forty minutes to reach Caro.

The Villa at Caro was more lavish than what Peiro had narrated. It was on top of a small hillock and gave panoramic views on all four sides. There were no boundary walls on any side, but there were no other buildings for miles. Sea was visible on three sides. The fourth side was lush forest which presently, due to winters, looked grey.

Rocky entered the beautifully decorated hall on one side of which was a well stocked bar. In the center was a wooden floor with a multitude of stage lights hanging from the roof. On one side stood the band ready to play. The place gave the look of a perfect night club.

Luigi sat on a bar stool with a highball of whisky. Behind the bar was a barman, but on this side of the bar besides Luigi, a couple of scantily dressed girls also stood. Rocky reached the bar, removed his jacket and sat next to him. Luigi signaled one of his attendants. He took away the jacket. They sat down discussing their next plans.

"How much is this?" Luigi asked.

"Eight kilograms!" Answered Rocky, "Just imagine I had to keep this on my body all through the journey."

"And now you will have to wear one and a half million dollars the same way! I wonder how it must be feeling to have so much of money around your body!"

"Not very pleasant, of course!" laughed Rocky. "It gives pleasure later!"

"But Rocky, we need to expand. I was hoping that you will find some more assistants to expand the business faster. But it seems you have fired even the existing ones."

"I did not develop enough confidence in them. I thought they were not fit for more serious or bigger jobs. But don't worry, I will soon find some good ones." Rocky said, "How big would be the next lot?"

"Will you be able to deliver twenty kilos by next month?"

"I guess so. But I am not sure of the price. Getting through Malaysia is only possible for me. And I have some other assignments waiting."

"Why don't you share your technique with some trusted assistant? Your business could grow four or five fold."

"Will do so, when the time comes."

The music had started. A young belly dancer appeared in the middle of the hall and the lights of different colours began dancing with her, accentuating her seducing movements. Rocky pulled one of the girls who was standing near him, and made her sit on another stool next to him. His left arm wound round her waist. He bent a little and reached for her lips. She too bent, but in such a way that her breasts came forward and face upwards. In making an effort to reach her lips, Rocky had to press hard against her breasts.

The gyrating belly dancer moved forward and reached so close to Rocky that he could hold her hand. But just as he was about to touch her, he froze in the middle. Across the wooden dance floor, stood Baadshaah. With his typical bloodshot cruel eyes and the cunning smile which was said to be a precursor to his devilish destructive actions. Rocky had no idea that Luigi and Baadshaah could be even knowing each other. Now that he was here, meant something entirely different. His million and half were gone for sure, but that was least of his concern. These could be his last moments on the earth. He wished he had found Bhure lal and cajoled him into continuing with this work. If it was Bhure lal, he would have been safe today. He reached his pocket to get a feel of the magic band. It was there. But Rocky knew in his heart, the band could be of no use if he was caught once. And now from the middle of this hall disappearing suddenly before getting caught was not going to be possible. Sweat beads appeared on his forehead. Baadshaah moved forward towards him.

18

Elizabeth had never seen such scenery live. She had been watching such pictures in coffee books and movies and had often thought that these places actually do not exist in nature. They are created in the studios by artists of highest caliber. She had lived in Mumbai during her childhood and Delhi later and had never been out of a city life on a holiday or even sightseeing trip. Nature meant to her Elephanta or Borivali national park or the Ridge or Tughlaqabad fort. Now she had been travelling in a car for about eight hours. They had crossed several small cities, towns, villages, lakes, rivers and jungles, and it was just awesome. Yes. She could not find any words to describe the beauty she had been watching. It would have been far more difficult to describe her feelings. It was probably a new life she had been totally unaware of. They were driving in a picturesque mountain road at a very high altitude. Every turn gave a glimpse of the deep valley thousands of feet below or white shining snow topped mountain peaks. It was cold but they were all enjoying the cold biting breeze. The sun was bright but except for the point where it fell, the heat did not traverse anywhere. The green jungles all around and scores of monkeys on both sides of the road, tiny cubs riding on the back of their mother were creating an indelible impression on her mind. She had forgotten the objective of her travel. She had also forgotten that the car was being driven by a driver and Hari sat on the passenger seat in the front row. It was just she immersed in her dreams sharing the back seat of the car with Shiv Prasad and going on and on, on a beautiful endless journey. Yes, she did not want it to end ever. She must not wake up from her dream ever!

But the car stopped. The driver said, "Sir, this is the best place to have lunch. Then we shall drive a further three – four hours before we reach. You may not find a better place in the next couple of hours."

It was a hill resort. Beautifully manicured garden with lots of flowers. There was a restaurant on the ground floor and some rooms on the upper floor. On one side was the thousands of feet deep valley and mountain on the other side. A narrow track moved up the hill. It was probably used by the tourists for trekking. Up on the hill there were a few huts.

About two hundred metres from the resort was a small natural water fall. A narrow wooden pathway had been made with steel railings up to the fall. From there, a small part of the falling water was diverted towards the resort like a narrow meandering ribbon. Inside the resort this took the form of a small pond and then flowed back towards the edge and then down into the valley.

Elizabeth went closer and saw ducks and red and yellow coloured fish in the pond. She walked up to the water fall and got the natural cold spray of water on her face. The water was ice cold and very refreshing. She stood there for a while allowing the water spray to wet her face and dress and finally wiped her face feeling rejuvenated.

There was a hammock tied between two trees. If she had time, she would have loved to lie down in the hammock with a novel.

There were some cars parked at the edge of the opening. They went right up to the edge of the cliff and looked around. There were no huts or any other signs of civilization anywhere. Whatever was there, was only at the resort where they stood.

Small wooden tables were placed out and people had been having their food. Some were walking around and taking pictures.

Hari told them that this was the most ideal place for trekking, watching the sunrise and exploring the wild life.

They all got down and sat around a table. The food was ordered. They were all hungry. The food was simple but tasted delicious. After the food they were still sitting at the table. The driver went a little away probably to have smoke. Hari too walked to the edge admiring the natural beauty.

Elizabeth suddenly blurted out, "We shall have our honey moon here!"

"Honeymoon? Are you getting married? You never gave an inkling!" Shiv Prasad exclaimed.

"No, no! I...I ... just.... I mean ... when I marry...." Stammered an embarrassed Elizabeth. But deep inside her heart, response of Shiv Prasad stung her. She became sad.

As if to her rescue, Hari returned. Blushing Elizabeth confined her gaze to the ground below, as if she was caught stealing.

Hari did not notice anything. He simply asked, "Shall we move? We still have a long way to go."

"Yes, of course!"

And they returned to the car and on to their lovely journey.

At about seven in the evening it had already become dark. Dim lights from small shops and huts seemed to be preparing for the night ahead. The village was small, calm and peaceful. The lone cows or donkeys on the road were the only obstructions.

They were soon on the outskirts of the village. A relatively large compound with wooden fence greeted them. It had no gate. They just drove in. There was a volleyball court with the net still in place. The hut had a verandah in the front lit by an electric bulb. Some children sat on the ground under the bulb studying. As the car drove in they all got up and circled around the car.

And soon there were loud excited announcements, "Oh Hari Bhaiya has come! Hari Bhaiya has come! …Mama, see! …..Papa! Look …….Hari Bhaiya! …Hari Bhaiya has come in a car!...."

The crowd encircled their beloved Hari Bhaiya and began taking him inside. Shiv Prasad and Elizabeth were probably not even noticed by the excited children. As they stood wondering what to do, a middle aged man and a woman emerged out of the hut. Hari quickly moved forward and bent down to touch their feet. The couple now saw Elizabeth and Shiv Prasad. Hari also invited them to come forward and occupy a charpoy in the verandah. The children ran in and brought out some chairs. The excited children would not leave Hari and their noise did not allow Hari to start any discussion with the hosts, not even tell the purpose of their visit! After about half an hour they could move on to some relatively noise free corner of the hut and begin discussion.

Shiv Prasad had, just after seeing the hut and the inmates, completely demolished his preconceived impression of Mr. India. Even before starting discussions, he was confident that this man could never be involved in any such thing. But yes, the possibility of his having told the secret of becoming invisible to someone did exist and that one little information could easily lead them to the culprit.

He did not know how to start. He wondered how to tell what brought him here. He wondered how this man would react if he came to know that he was suspecting him to be the terrorist. He began asking about the children.

"These are children of poor parents who either don't have enough resources to feed them or look after them, or don't have the approval of the society for doing the same! So, I get benefitted! They become my children. My home is always full of children's lovely noise. There is always life, happenings, happiness! These children have made my life worth living!" Anil said.

"But how do you get the money for feeding them?" Shiv Prasad had not thought that it will be so easy to start probing into his sources of income.

"See, we have these farms, where I, Sridevi and older children work. Then the villagers also help. And now, several of my children like Hari have grown up and have started earning. They keep sending money! Our needs are very limited. We never faced any financial problems!" He laughed.

A teenager girl brought some hot pakoras and tea for them.

Shiv Prasad bit into one of the pakoras and came to the prime purpose of his visit. He narrated the whole story, the murder on Akbar road, the statement of Bhure lal and the sinister plan Bhure lal thought was being planned by this Aidni RM.

Anil became very serious. He said, "My Dad had invented this gadget. The gadget, when worn round the left hand wrist, makes the person invisible. But then he thought that it could be misused by unscrupulous persons. So he kept it hidden. I found it and used it to help the police bust the terrorist gang. By the time the terrorist gang was busted, I had realized that this gadget could be very dangerous for mankind. I did not want anyone to get this and so I had thrown it in the sea. I don't think anyone could have got this. But if someone has been able to get another one made, then definitely, it is not good. And like you say, if someone with a destructive frame of mind gets it, then it can be worse than disastrous.

"Now I don't know how we can catch this person or how we can stop him. Frankly, as you might be seeing, I am a very simple villager and can't think of anything more serious than the pranks of these children.

"But this is one matter where I know it is my duty to do everything that can be done. You tell me what I can do, and I will do it."

Once again a dead end, thought Shiv Prasad. "Okay, since you have used this gadget extensively, may be you can tell me some loopholes, some methods by which it can be made ineffective!"

"Yes, of course!" Joyfully exclaimed Anil, "you may be remembering how I was caught by those gangsters - don't you?"

Shiv Prasad looked at him blankly.

"The invisible person can be seen in red light. They switched on all red lights in the building and I could not hide from them! If you want to catch this man, get him in a room and switch on all red lights. He will be caught."

Shiv Prasad's eyes brightened. Yes it was well nigh impossible to lure this fellow in to a room and get red lights switched on. But at least now something could be thought of. There was some light at the end of this tunnel.

They kept on discussing ways and means of catching this criminal till late into the night. Hari was not let free by the children and he could not participate in any of the discussions. But in the morning when they were about to leave, he was relieved to see the admiration and respect for Anil and Sridevi in the eyes of Shiv Prasad and Elizabeth. His joy knew no bound when they both bent down to touch their feet before getting into the car.

19

"I am sure before entering into this line, you knew what happens to those who ditch in the middle of some operation or try to quit!" With his menacing voice and cunning smile, Baadshaah slowly moved towards Rocky.

His mouth dried up. He exactly knew what happens. But what he did not know was that it happens so quickly. And the irony was that he was not really trying to quit or ditch him. He had every intention of completing the job. He was completely geared up. It was only his accomplice who had developed cold feet and he had been punished. Within hours of his failure. But how to convince Baadshaah of his clear intentions?

He tried to bring composure to his face. Making his voice as calm as he could in the face of his impending termination. He said, "Look Baadshaah, You should be aware of the odds against which we work. When after thousands of checks and tests the space missions fail, why our mission which is developed and is proposed to be implemented practically alone, with the help of just two or three untrained amateurs, can't fail?"

He was himself surprised at the coolly delivered well balanced and logical little speech. He paused to gauge the effect of his speech and once he realized that it was having the desired effect, he started again, "I had everything lined up. It was a very thin line of action which broke. Unfortunately, in our line of business these thin lines play such important roles that they can make or mar the mission. My handy man who messed up, has been rewarded suitably with three bullets through his heart." He paused again to see the reaction.

The music had stopped and there was complete silence. The belly dancer stood on a side waiting for something to happen.

"I have not ditched you. My first effort has failed. And it's just that! Unfortunately in order to complete the job, we have to wait for one full year. No other similar opportunity is possible before that." Rocky paused again.

"If you wish, you may have your advance payment back and the deal is dead. Else, have patience, wait for one year and get the result you wanted." He was emboldened by the silent acceptance of his statements.

Baadshaah at last spoke, "Look! Ala kamaan had been eagerly waiting for this action to take place. You will not believe, Ala kamaan himself sat watching the complete stupid show and he was so crest fallen at the end watching them getting into their cars and returning that he called me immediately and asked me to bring your head."

A cold shiver ran through the spine of Rocky.

"You may please pacify Ala kamaan to have some patience. We cannot rush the things too fast. You remember how long you had to wait before attacking Mumbai? And that was a small operation as compared to the one I am undertaking." He looked around to see the effect again.

"Remember, this operation is possible only by me. Out of the seven billion people in the world, there is but just this one man who has the competence to do it. You may kill me and then never have this operation done. Or you may wait and get this done next year. The choice is yours."

Confident that he had won the argument, he casually turned, picked up his glass of whisky from the bar counter, gulped it, and began walking out. Then he paused and turned to Luigi, "Am I having my jacket, or this was the last deal with you?"

Luigi too picked up his glass and gulped it. "What is the hurry? Your flight leaves in the morning. We have several hours with us." And he signaled the band to restart. The atmosphere again began reverberating with the beats of the Arabian music and the swinging and shaking of the belly dancer's breasts and hips.

Baadshaah moved closer to Rocky, pulled a stool and sat across him. "Look Rocky, Ala kamaan will not be happy with this. He is not likely to be sitting idle and waiting endlessly. Till we get to the final show, there must be some small fireworks."

"Now you are talking!" Rocky had piled up lots of confidence in the past few minutes. "But you are talking like a Kinder Garten kid. These actions are not crackers you fire after winning a cricket match. These have to be seriously thought over, meticulously planned and then executed with patience and courage.

"And if in your hurry, you screw up a poorly chalked out plan, you won't have the grand finale Ala Kamaan is so eagerly waiting for.

"Give me time. I will come up with something bright. But don't rush things up, don't get impatient...... and don't ever talk to me in that tone!" He was amazed at his own courage. He slipped his hand in his pocket and felt the wrist band. Thanked it again – all the courage stemmed out of its magic! He smiled in his heart.

20

Shiv Prasad reviewed the security arrangements of Bhure Lal. He was in a small cabin on the third floor of the hospital. There was no possibility of anyone entering from the window. The only door had two constables on watch. But he could not be sure of these two constables. Plus, in this case the situation was more tricky than dangerous. The attacker could come invisible to the common eye. He may just find the door open and the constables wide awake fully alert. And he may just casually walk in and fire at the patient and walk away as coolly as he had come!

He asked the attending doctor the condition of his patient. He said that the wound had healed and he could go home. They were only waiting for the clearance from the police department. He advised him to retain the patient and issue a report that the patient had developed some complications and had to be kept in hospital longer. He then called in the hospital electrical maintenance person and told him to replace the existing fluorescent tube light with a red light bulb. He advised the constables to ensure that the red bulb was kept switched on at all times.

Elizabeth had been silently watching all the instructions Shiv Prasad was passing. Now she appeared a little uncomfortable. Shiv Prasad noticed it and looked at her questioningly.

She said, "I am afraid Aidni Rm may not come if he sees the red lights on. I am sure he too knows that his guise would become ineffective in red light. So he would rather not take a chance and wait for some better opportunity. I think the red light should not be prominent. It should be conspicuously placed, so as to catch him unaware." She paused and said again, "Can we not have some gadget which would sense an ingress and activate an alarm?"

Shiv Prasad looked impressed. He thought for a while and then asked her to get in touch with the electronics department to find and install such a device in his room. Then he sat down with Bhure Lal to know more about the modus operandi of this Aidni Rm.

Elizabeth had found out about the mobile phone recovered from Bhure lal. Surprisingly, from this phone also, all communications were confined to one single number. And from that single number, two mobiles were in touch. The other number probably belonged to Pratap, they concluded. Hence the criminal had very intelligently developed a closed loop of communication. He kept several mobile phones, switched on one only when required and contacted only one number from it. So no one could reach the other accomplices through the mobile phone numbers. In between he made contacts through slips which said nothing more than "contact at so and so hours!" His plans were kept so close to his chest that his own men could not get any idea of what they had to do, until they were about to do it. There was an imperative need to understand well how this man operated and what could be his next mission. Apparently he was targeting VVIPs and for him getting into South Block was almost as simple as walking into metro at Central Secretariat!

He asked Bhure lal all the jobs he had performed for this guy. It turned out that Bhure Lal was only being used as a courier for drugs. He himself did not know what he was actually doing. He was ordered to go to some point and collect a bag or deliver a bag. He was not supposed to open it or ask what was in it. He was given a code word with which the other party recognized him and carried out the deal.

He had been travelling abroad also. Generally Italy, France, Spain, Portugal etc. Pratap was being sent to eastern side. Singapore, Malaysia, Myanmar, even Australia. But he too was doing the same jobs without knowing what he was carrying. They were handed over the bag they had to carry, a passport and some foreign exchange just a few hours before the flight. They were also told what to answer when they were questioned. But their stay abroad always limited to two or three days.

They were given plenty of money but were not allowed to go home. Pratap used to go to his home and he would go to Pratap's home to deliver money.

But last month Pratap was given a very serious assignment. He was sent to Peshawar without any bag to deliver. He met a local man there and with him travelled very long distances in Pakistan and arrived at a town called Kasur near the border. They went right upto the fencing at a point where there were no army personnel, threw an AK47 rifle far into the fencing and returned. Two days later he went to Ferozepur and then drove to the same place from Indian side with a long fishing rod and fished the rifle out. He then carried that rifle with him to Delhi in a small air bag with his dirty clothes. This gun was to be handed over to Aidni Rm near Meridien Hotel on the 26th.

Both Pratap and Bhure Lal had never seen this man but had talked to him several times on the phone and even directly. The man could move objects, pick up a gun or bags and also make them disappear. Since he was invisible, they were always scared that he might be present around and listening to what they were talking.

Bhure Lal could not give any more information, but whatever he told was important and helpful for planning his next course of action. One more very important information he gave was that on the day he got fired upon, he was supposed to call him in the afternoon. Probably he had to travel on that day, because such messages usually were given for travelling to other countries. But he had no idea as to where he would have been asked to go or if at all really he had to go.

Shiv Prasad returned to his office and began discussing with Elizabeth. They concluded that either some delivery had to be given or taken. After Pratap deserted him, he was not sure of Bhure Lal and wanted to eliminate him. At the same time since this appointment had to be honoured, he planted Ankit to kill him and himself left to complete the work. That explained why he had so long not attacked Bhure Lal again.

But now he should be returning, since these people always returned in two-three days. Now the risk of attack on Bhure Lal was growing. Through this discussion, they also reached one more possibility of rounding up this man. He would be returning to India from some foreign country. If proper surveillance is carried out at the airport, it may be easy to nab him there before he proceeds to either kill Bhure Lal or any other important person. The more important issue was how to see him at the airport. It was impossible to turn all the airport lights to red. In ordinary lights he would just walk out without creating a flutter.

Elizabeth suddenly picked up a pen from the pen holder on the desk of Shiv Prasad. It was actually a laser pointer which he used in presentations to show a particular point to the audience. She pressed the button and waved the pointer in all directions. Then with a winning smile explained, "Sir, give these pointers to some plainclothesmen at the airport. They may keep waving this pointer aimlessly in all directions but watch very carefully where the point gets projected. Normally the point would fall on the farthest object falling directly on the path of this light. But if this Aidni Rm is standing anywhere in the middle, the light would fall on him and not pass through to the farther object. Once they get a suspicion, they may silently follow this object which is not visible but blocks the red laser beam. They may then message other colleagues in the vicinity and surround and capture this guy. For the sake of convenience, they may be equipped with red light torches also."

Shiv Prasad was impressed. His admiring look once again made Elizabeth to blush. But in a flash the joy was again overpowered by the deep seated sting in her heart.

21

Peiro dropped him at the Flumicino Airport, also known as Leonardo Da Vinci Airport. The entire route was covered in silence. Rocky was very sleepy, but still could not sleep. He was recounting all the happenings of the evening. He had indeed come out unscathed, but things were difficult. He had lost two of his important lieutenants. One major job would be to find substitutes for them. That means travelling in small towns and spending time in third grade restaurants or college canteens. Suitable people had to be screened from these places only who would follow his diktat unquestioningly, be happy with the money he was paying and not have enough courage to divulge whatever little they came to know about him. But searching such people was not easy. He would have to follow prospective candidates for a few days before making the first efforts to woo them.

He was also worried over what might have happened to Bhure Lal. The way he had brainwashed Ankit, it was sure to work. He must have fired at Bhure Lal if he made any effort to come back in the apartment. But may be he did not come. Even this would be OK so long as he does not go to the police and starts spilling the beans. What if he comes and Ankit develops cold feet? As the time is passing this possibility is getting stronger. His instructions would keep getting fainter and Ankit would get more reassured and carefree. But if Bhure did not return within a week, he may never return.

Once again he felt reassured that Bhure Lal anyway did not know much about him to cause harm. But he did not want to take any chances.

Another important work that was left incomplete and would be a serious cause of concern was picking up the AK47 from the Apartment. He felt sorry that he did not pick it up when he had taken Ankit there. But then the problem was keeping it. He did not want to keep it in his own home. Shailaja knew that he was involved in some illegal activities, but an AK47 would be far beyond her comprehension. Additionally, he did not want to be carrying it when he was not invisible. The whole thing must be planned. Planned meticulously. Unfortunately the last week had been too hectic. He did not get any opportunity to sit down calmly and think logically. But now, and during the flight he would develop a concrete plan of action and sort out each of the issues.

Rocky stood in the driveway watching Peiro drive out his Porsche. Then he casually moved in to the terminal building. He looked at the flights leaving for Delhi. It was leaving in about an hour from gate number 43. He walked in to the toilet. In his usual composed manner, he took out the wrist band, kissed it, slipped it on his left wrist and watched his wrist disappear in thin air. He had not bolted the door of the WC. The door was still ajar. He walked out as casually as he had walked in, and moved on to the security enclosure.

Here things were difficult. There was a fairly large crowd. Passengers were removing their shoes, belts, keys and wallets, putting their mobiles in the hand baggage, taking out their laptops and placing them on a separate tray and then walking in to the small cubicle, where they had to stand with feet exactly on the mark and hands raised up. The electronic door moved and they could move on. On the other side again they had to put back on their shoes, belts, stow the laptop back into the bag and take out their wallets before moving on. All the bags and trays were being put on trays and passing through an x-ray machine over a conveyor belt. The empty trays were being recycled back over the X-ray machine block.

Rocky waited for a while and caught a small moment when the top of the X-ray machine was empty. He jumped on to the machine and then on the other side. But in this exercise, he tripped a small tray with coins and a wrist watch which lay over the machine. The tray fell spreading the coins all over. The lady sitting next to the x-ray machine looking intently at her monitor turned around to see how and what fell, could see the coins on the floor, but could not figure out how it could have fallen. She turned her gaze to the passengers who could have pushed it, but the nearest passenger was far enough to have pushed it. She swore in inaudible words and got back to her work.

The passenger whose coins had fallen, began arguing with the security personnel on the way they had been treating passengers. Rocky moved on to the gate 43, where boarding was about to be announced.

Once again he tailed the last passenger boarding and got into the aircraft looking around for some vantage seat. The aircraft was relatively full. He walked till end and stood near the aft toilets. Aircraft door was about to be closed. He had been awake the whole night and badly wanted a shot of whisky before getting down to sleep. In the crowded plane staying invisible was more dangerous. Anybody could get the feel of his presence.

He hid behind the partition and removed his wrist band. Putting it in his pocket, he walked to the row where a young south Indian girl sat alone on the window seat. He occupied the vacant aisle seat next to her. She looked at him unhappily. He feigned indifference, spread his legs and closed his eyes. Just then he saw the air hostess walking down the aisle with the counter in her palm.

He had landed in to a problem. He sat silently thinking fast on how to set things right again. The hostess reached her station and tallied the count. Apparently there was a mismatch. She checked the papers again and the reading on the counter and then discussed with her colleague. Now the colleague took the counter and was about to start when Rocky got up again and went back to the aft toilets. He slid the wrist band again and walked back to the seat.

The hostess finished her counting and returned to her station. The discrepancy had disappeared. Both girls seemed happy and got busy with their chores. The plane had started moving backwards. Rocky went back to the toilet, removed the wrist band and returned to his seat again.

Soon after take off, he asked for his double whisky shot and in no time plunged into deep sleep. Rest of the journey was event free. As soon as the plane came to a halt at Delhi, without waiting for the seat belt sign to be switched off he ran to the aft toilet as if he had been controlling his pressure for a long time. In spite of the announcement of the hostess to return to seat, he rushed into the toilet, and stayed there until the passengers started disembarking. As they had been disembarking, no one was near these toilets. He slipped on his wrist band and began walking behind the last passenger.

At Delhi, he had no baggage to collect, so ignoring the baggage collection conveyor belts, he moved on towards the exit. But suddenly he stopped. A small red dot of light fell on his jacket. He looked at it unbelievingly. His rest of the body was invisible, but that point was on his jacket. He looked around to find the source of this light and saw a middle aged person sitting on a chair not far from him had a small laser pointer through which he was pointing the light on him and watching him intently.

The appearance of the man made him suspicious. He had very much a police look. But what he might be doing with the laser pointer in the arrival hall? And how come he was looking so intently at him as if he was able to see him?

Rocky got scared. Probably the effect of the wrist band has worn off. But he was still not able to see himself. He decided it was not good to take any chances. He looked around to find the signboard for a toilet and then quickly moved towards it. He did not wait for anyone to open the door, but opened himself and walked in and then into the nearest WC. He sure had panicked, but he did not have the time to calmly think and develop a strategy. Now the concern was saving his life.

He lowered the seat and sat down thinking on his next move and then decided to move on. He removed his wrist band and moved out of the toilet. His fears were not without basis. He thanked his wits for the quick corrective action he had taken.

There were now two plainclothes men, obviously police men, with similar laser pointers. They were moving their pointers in all directions carefully scanning the entire space at the exit of the toilets.

Rocky casually walked out without paying any attention to them. Now the next problem had cropped up. He had no passport or any other documents. His jacket had a million and a half dollars in different pockets and lining. He had to get out of the terminal building quickly without attracting any attention. He saw the south Indian girl near whom he had taken the seat in the plane, had collected her baggage and was pushing her trolley with two average sized bags and an airbag. He followed her keeping a distance of about fifteen feet.

As he began passing through the green channel, one of the customs officer asked for the customs slip. He quickly pointed to the girl walking fifteen feet ahead, and said, "Oh, it's with her – she just now handed it to you!"

The officer turned to look at the girl and Rocky swiftly moved on and walked out of the terminal building. But he was still not comfortable. He looked back over his shoulder, then, instead of coming out, went to the stair case and walked up to the departure level of the terminal. Here he saw an old couple getting out of a taxi. The driver was taking out their bags from the boot. He went to the driver, handed him a five hundred rupee note, and said in a hurried tone, "*Bhai sahib*, I have to quickly go home and get my passport. I can't wait in the line for taxi. Please drop me at Dhaula Kuan."

Taxi driver was more pleased than Rocky himself! He was getting Rupees five hundred, and a quick passenger without having to wait for a minute! Within a few seconds the taxi was zooming out of the terminal.

22

"Sir, I saw this man, I swear!" The constable told Shiv Prasad.

From the description he gave of how the laser was getting obstructed only in a limited width, and how it kept moving towards the toilet, made Shiv Prasad confident that the constable had indeed seen him. He had acted very correctly as per the brief given to him. He had followed the man till toilet, called his other colleague who was manning the other side in a similar manner and then both of them had kept a vigil over the exit of the toilet. When no one similar incident took place, they decided to go inside the toilet and search, but could not find the invisible man.

"Apparently, the man went in, removed his camouflage and walked out like any other ordinary passenger." Shiv Prasad said.

"Sir, let's screen the passengers who walked into the toilet and who came out during this period, through the CCTV." Suggested Elizabeth.

Shiv Prasad was getting more and more impressed with her intelligence with every passing day. They asked the airport security in-charge to give the CCTV recordings for the particular area covering two hours during which this incident took place and sat down with their eyes glued to the computer monitor.

It did not take them long to find that one passenger with a stylish slightly oversized jacket never went into the toilet but had come out of it. Unfortunately, he had been walking behind a tall man and his face was most of the time downwards. So the camera could not take a good shot at his face. But now they had some idea of the built and appearance of the person.

They called for other footages to track the entire route followed by the person. At the main exit they saw that he was stopped by the customs man, but he indicated towards someone walking ahead and had hurriedly followed him. They checked the footage again to see who was walking ahead of this person. There seemed to be a young south Indian lady moving with a trolley. Was she with him? She had two bags and an airbag. May be one belonged to this person.

They took printouts of both the lady and the suspected man. Incidentally, the picture of the woman was clear enough as she had stopped to hand over the customs slip to the man. But picture of the man was blurred since he did not stop. Further, his face was mostly down wards. CCTV coverage was not good enough beyond this point so it was not possible to find whether the two of them moved together or separately. How and where the man went beyond this point could not be found. They could only confirm that he had gone out in a large sized leather jacket without any baggage. Shiv Prasad believed the woman was not with him. He had only used her to distract the attention of the customs man.

Now the issue facing them was how to track the man. Once again he was in Delhi, he was free, and in all probability, would soon be striking. Shiv Prasad asked Elizabeth to pass on the photograph to the Passport Office to check if any passport was issued to him. Though he believed he was travelling on a fake passport. He also asked her to request the immigration authorities to compare the photograph with all passengers travelling out of Delhi after the date when Ankit had heard his inner voice and had returned on the date of this man's return.

Having passed these instructions, Shiv Prasad began discussing other possibilities. "One of his priorities would be to kill Bhure Lal. I think that is one place where he is sure to come and come soon. If we carefully lay a trap, we may be successful." Shiv Prasad said.

"I guess he does not know that Bhure lal is alive and in the hospital. He may probably go to the apartment to assess the situation and see if Ankit is still there." Elizabeth said.

"Should we free Ankit and ask him to return to the apartment?"

"That may work or may not work. Given that Ankit is mentally not very sound, I think that will be a big risk.

"It may be better if he sees the seal put by the police and tries to find out all that happened.

Then when he realizes that Bhure Lal is not dead, he may come to the hospital."

"Do the neighbours know what happened there and that Bhure Lal is in a hospital? I think Bhure Lal was not keeping any social contacts there and no one may be keeping a track of what was happening there."

There was a silence for a couple of minutes.

"We have once again reached a dead end." Shiv Prasad was visibly upset, "The only option we have is to closely monitor everything near the apartment and the hospital. We cannot rule out the possibility of his being absolutely indifferent to Bhure Lal's statements to police, considering that Bhure Lal really did not know almost anything about him, but besides that sole lead, we have nothing on our hands. We can probably just watch him commit the next crime, invisibly, right before our eyes."

"Liz, get me a constable's uniform!" He asked Elizabeth after a few moments, "If there is only one way, Shiv Prasad will not leave that one way unattended!"

23

Rocky got down at Dhaula Kuan, left the taxi and walked on the pavement for a while. Then he hailed another taxi and asked him to take him to AIIMs. From AIIMs he walked down to the adjoining Kidwai Nagar and called Shailaja to pick him up. He walked in to INA market and aimlessly began window shopping.

Shailaja arrived in about twenty minutes and then they were home in about fifteen minutes. He was tired, but more than physical fatigue, he was mentally disturbed. Shailaja looked at him and understood, asking anything now or even initiating a dialogue would be inviting trouble. She brought a double shot of blue label, silently put it on the table in front of him and left.

Rocky liked this understanding of his girlfriend. She knew exactly when to ask something, when to crib, and when to remain completely silent. He had to decide his priorities. The way the two cops had been trying to nab him had made him nervous. The most troubling part was how the red spot showed up on his jacket.

He went to the dressing room attached to his bedroom, took out the wrist band from his pocket, took off the jacket and safely hung it in between other clothes in the wardrobe. Then he slipped the wrist band on his left wrist and saw it disappear. He looked into the drawer and found a laser pointer. He focused it on himself and was aghast to see it showed on him. It would be so easy to trace his outline through the laser reaching farther at points where he did not exist and getting stopped where he stood. Now the more serious point was how the cops had come to know of this secret?

He slipped out of the house and into the garage. He switched on the tail lights and stood there and his worst fears came true. He was clearly visible in red light. So somehow the police had come to know that he would be visible in red light and had laid the trap at the airport. They also knew that he was arriving at the airport. Is the game over? He did not think Bhure Lal had discovered these things and had enlightened the police. He did not appear to be so smart or intelligent.

Nevertheless, he will have to find out whether he is still alive and if he is, how much he knows. There was no time to sleep now. He had to find the facts for his survival. He took out the wrist band, went in the house and told Shailaja that he was again going out and may remain out for a few days. Shailaja obviously did not like it, but preferred not to comment.

He went out and took a taxi to Geeta Colony.

At Geeta Colony, he went to a secluded corner, waited for some time to ensure that no one was about to come and then slipped on the wrist band. Then he walked out, walking slowly, and hiding quickly behind any available cover to avoid the tail lights of passing cars. He was soon at the apartment where he had left Ankit a few days ago. Near the apartment, on the street sat on a stool, a lone constable, half dozing. Probably Bhure has been killed. He thought.

He passed twice in front of the constable. His position did not change. Encouraged, he walked up the stairs and found the police seal on the door. He heaved a sigh of relief. He was satisfied to a large extent, but the questions that had cropped up in his mind today after the airport incident, remained unanswered. He began his return walk but once outside the lane, his curiosity took the better of him.

He slipped out the wrist band and walked to a boy standing near a shop. He gave him a fifty rupee note and asked him to go up to the apartment and see if anyone was there. If there was no one, he should ask anyone nearby where the person had gone. He could tell he wanted to see his friend Ankit.

The boy looked a little puzzled but a fifty rupee note coming his way so easily kept his mouth shut. The unsuspecting boy ran to the apartment. Rocky slipped on his wrist band and came closer to the apartment to be able to watch and listen whatever happened there. As the boy touched the seal on the door of the apartment, the constable came to life.

"Hey! What do you want?" He roared.

The boy sure did not expect to be confronting a police man.

"No, nothing." He said and tried to run away.

But the police man who had been dozing till a few minutes ago conjured up the swiftness of a fox in a flash, jumped and caught hold of the boy's hand.

"Tell me what were you trying to do?"

"No, *sahib*! Nothing. One man asked me to see if anyone was living here. So I came to check. See he gave me fifty rupees." He showed the note to the police man.

"Where is the man? Show me." He did not leave the boy's hand and began walking with him to the shop where Rocky had met him.

Reaching the spot the boy said, "Sahib he seems to have left."

Boy's father came out of the shop and asked what was going on. The Constable without leaving the boy's hand said, "He was trying to enter the house where last week a man was murdered. This house is sealed and anybody trying to enter has to be arrested."

"But he was not trying to enter. Somebody asked him to check and he had only gone to check. You catch the person who asked him to check." His father said in an aggressive tone.

"Nobody is here. He is telling lies."

"No, I heard his voice. He was here, but has gone now after seeing that you have caught him." Argued the father, "He is innocent. Catch the culprit not innocent citizens."

Shiv Prasad was confident that Aidni Rm was around in his invisible form. He was tempted to take out the little laser pointer and catch him. But in case he was not close enough, that would give him an easy escape, and the opportunity which seemed to be within reach would be lost again.

He looked around as if ensuring that no one was around and then said in hushed tone to the father, "Actually it is top secret. There was a terrorist hiding here. The man is not dead but he is very seriously injured. He is being treated in the Government hospital here. Police fears that his accomplices will kill him and they will not be able to get his statement. That is why we have to be careful. I know this kid is innocent. I think the man who asked him to find was the real terrorist. He has run away now. He needs to be caught." He looked around again, but no one was in sight.

He left the boy's hand, then said, "It's already past ten. My reliever has not yet come. I am hungry and sleepy. Please do me a favour, if the supervisor comes here, just tell him that I have just gone next door for a tea. I will be back in ten minutes."

He did not know whether Aidni Rm still stood there or not, but to make the story sound real, he had to make up some such excuse before leaving the place.

He moved away. He had a fear that if Aidni Rm followed him, his story would be caught. But there appeared to be little reason for Aidni Rm to follow him. Once he was reasonably far, he took out the mobile from his pocket and called Elizabeth, "Liz, we are in luck. I guess the prey would be near the bait soon."

....

Rocky heaved a sigh of relief. Once again his intuition had saved him from impending disaster. A look at this dozing constable had activated the alarm bells in his mind. The man did not appear to be an ordinary constable on duty. He was alert and pretending to be dozing off. The suspicion had gathered strength when he caught the boy with incredible swiftness. Finally his leaking the secret information without anyone seeking it and then leaving the duty point with a lame excuse! Anyone with a careful, alert and logical mind could have seen through the ploy.

Delhi Police still has to find competent personnel to catch him! He smiled in his heart, and left for home. His questions were not answered and probably he would have to live for a long period before getting those answers, but hurrying now was straight away falling into one of the traps, however sloppy they may be! He would go back now and plan leisurely, while the cops sweat and wear themselves out! Going to a secluded place, he removed his wrist band and hailed a taxi for Connaught place.

24

The cabin where Bhure Lal lied, had a new gadget installed. This was a simple thief alarm across the door. On one side was a source of a thin laser band and on the other side a sensor. As soon as anyone crossed this door, the sensor would get a break and would activate the alarm. A switch was on the bedside of Bhure Lal, through which he could deactivate the alarm for anyone seeking entry. Outside, a little away were a couple of police constables armed with torches flashing red lights.

Shiv Prasad was waiting in the small police office on the ground floor of the hospital. He was sure the attacker would make his attempt tonight. He waited the whole night but nothing abnormal happened. He finally called Elizabeth, "Liz, I am afraid I goofed up. When I was talking to you, he was listening. He won't come now. At least over the next few days. We have to find a different strategy." He hung up and got up to return home, tired and dejected.

25

Rocky returned to his home. His problems did not seem to be ending. To add to his worries, the police had not only become aware of his ability to become invisible, but also an easy way to see him when he was supposed to be invisible. His whole plan seemed to be shattering. Now should he lie low for some time? How long? But the retailers would soon be on his neck. The retail business had to continue and for that supplies had to continue. With Pratap dead and Bhure Lal out of circulation, he had to either operate himself or quickly find a substitute for these two jokers. After seeing how the police was trying to trap him in Geeta Colony, and how they were scanning the airport with laser pointers it would be suicidal for him to start operating himself.

He began a mental search out of the retailing crew for the potential candidates for taking up the position of Pratap and Bhure Lal. None of them appeared to be fitting for these positions. In any case, he did not know them too well. A new search had to be started.

He locked himself up in his study. The study was a small room well isolated from all sides, giving him full privacy. It had just a table and a chair and one single seat relaxing sofa where he could even sleep with legs spread out, like in the first class in an aircraft. The table had several computers, mobile phones, sim cards and data cards, all neatly labeled with unique identification tags. The labels did not give any indication of what they meant. Only Rocky could decipher them. He switched on one of the mobiles. Soon sms's began pouring in. He read them. All were from his retailers seeking supplies. It was natural. The supplies had been suspended for quite a few days.

He switched off the mobile and switched on another one. He did not expect any message in this one. He had already given Baadshaah a very clear indication of what could be expected now and in how many days. There should not be any message from his side. But it was their understanding that the messages would be checked at least twice every week.

To his horror, a message with a red flag appeared as soon as the mobile could locate a net work. He opened it. Baadshaah wanted him to call him any day between 11 and 11.10 pm within next three days. He looked at his watch. There were still a couple of minutes left to 11.10 pm. His intuition said the matter is important. But he was not prepared to take any important message now. He had to organize his own system first. He had to plan his strategy. Lot of work was pending. He decided to call him the next day. In any case he avoided calling from his home. He would move to a location few kilometers away and then only call.

He switched off the mobile and switched on the third one. One of his suppliers in Nepal was ready with a delivery. He switched off and checked his mails also. There were similar cryptic messages from the same sources. He wrote a one line mail, "call at 8 pm tomorrow", then switched off and moved to the sofa. Raised the foot rest to almost horizontal position, reclined the back to about thirty degrees, closed his eyes and began thinking.

One comforting factor was that the police had not actually seen him. So he could move about freely as an ordinary man. But getting into trouble for a petty thing like taking delivery of minuscule amounts or passing it on to retailers was not worth the risk. He would lie low, spending time with Shailaja! He had promised her before going to Italy that he would be having some free time. Well, he was now being forced to have this free time.

He got up and moved towards the bed room, but stopped midway. An alarm bell rang in his mind, 'never underestimate your enemy'. This police officer was stupid enough to have failed in this mission, but he was still pretty smart to have found out his secrets. Without knowing about this gadget, he had discovered that it was ineffective in red light. A fact that he himself did not know although he had been using this gadget for about two years. God knows what else he knows and what he has already made public. This guy is dangerous and must be taken care. Rocky did not want to take the police head on, but there seemed to be no options. His last mission failed because of the stupidity of his assistant. Next must not fail because of the smartness of a cop. Or his own complacence. Something must be done. He got into the bed with his head still struggling to find the next step. Shailaja's subtle attempts to arouse him went unnoticed, and finally she decided not to disturb him any further and end up getting admonished. Getting cold shouldered was better. She thought wryly.

26

Shiv Prasad sat in his usual "deep thinking" posture with both elbows on the table and palms covering eyes and forehead. Elizabeth sat silently on the side of the huge table drawing arbitrary lines on her pad. The coffee after having spread its aroma in the room, was lying cold and neglected in the mug.

"I am worried that we have as yet no idea of his intentions. Or rather, we know the intentions, but don't know how and when he may implement his plans. Unfortunately, he now knows that we know his secret of being visible in red light. We may now install red lights at all vulnerable points. Can we put red lights every where? On the streets? In the compounds? For all the VVIPs? All over the country? And he will see these from a distance and will never come closer. OK, if he doesn't come closer, the VVIPs are safe, but then we don't get to catch him. He may keep waiting for the right opportunity.

"Now look at another angle. These red lights will work during night. During day, in broad sunshine, do you think your red torches or laser pointers will have any effect? This guy may just walk up to the VVIP getting out from his car after a function and shoot." He waited for a while and said, "And we don't have a lead or a clue!"

He remained silent for a few seconds and then began again, "OK, Let's see how many loose ends we have left unattended in the case.

"First the revolver we recovered from Ankit. We made no effort to find out to whom did it belong to.

"Second, we have not checked to whom did this apartment belong to. Aidni Rm had probably taken it on rent. He must have entered into an agreement with the owner or given his identity. We have not even questioned his neighbours who might have noticed people coming in or going out.

"Third, we have not paid any attention to the other likely contacts of Aidni Rm. He was into drug business. Some people must be supplying him and some must be taking deliveries from him. The smaller operators. We should question Bhure Lal more on these aspects."

"Fourth, though we could not find how Pratap had been travelling abroad, we could have questioned Bhure Lal more about it. He must at least be remembering whether he was travelling in his own name or some assumed name."

He paused and Elizabeth interjected, "Another point we must ponder about, is, how this guy Aidni Rm picked up Ankit. Ankit does not seem to have anything to do with drug business. Aidni Rm suddenly found him on the street and began directing him. It can not be such a simple case. Aidni Rm must have watched him and zeroed in on him before picking him up for his job. Hence we may ask what exactly had Ankit been doing before he began hearing his 'inner voice'."

Shiv Prasad thought about it, and said, "Yes let us begin from Ankit only. In the mean time, send a message to find the owner of the revolver."

He suddenly became silent. He had noticed the curtain move slightly out of rhythm. The natural movement of the curtain because of the fan had been different. No reasons could be attributed to this out of rhythm movement. Shiv

Prasad's all senses were suddenly on maximum alert but he did not want this alertness to be evident from his appearance or actions. He had also become very tense.

Elizabeth began to say something, but he almost shouted, "Please do not disturb me. Let me think calmly."

It was too rude. Elizabeth could not believe her ears. Shiv Prasad had never spoken to her in that tone. She looked up at his face, trying to understand what had gone wrong. Nothing could be read from his face. He again said in a very annoying tone. "Liz, please leave me alone for some time. You are disturbing me."

Elizabeth got up and dashed out trying to control her tears. She threw the note pad and pencil on her table, hid her face in her arms, resting the head on the table and began sobbing uncontrollably.

"That was pretty smart of you, Shiv Prasad!" A voice from nowhere came. Shiv Prasad looked up guessing the direction from where the sound came. His hand began slowly moving towards the drawer. The voice came again, "Don't even try to do that, Shiv Prasad! Please raise both your hands above your head and keep sitting without a move."

Shiv Prasad raised his hands above his head, his mind racing fast to find next possible moves. The voice came again, "As I said, you very smartly moved your stupid secretary to safety! Alas, you won't be able to move yourself to safety!" The voice paused and came again, "You might have realized by now that you have only few minutes to live. I have both a good news and a bad news for you! The bad news is that the duration of your remaining life may be further shortened if you make any wrong move like try to get the gun out of that drawer. The good news is that those minutes may be longer if you co-operate – stay absolutely still and just answer my questions."

The voice continued, "I know you are trying to guess my location so that you may pounce upon me or hit me with something. Let me tell you, this would be futile. It will just reduce your life by a few more minutes. And just don't be under any illusion that after killing you I won't be able to run away. I have surveyed your office quite nicely and know exactly what to do, where to hide and finally escape without being seen."

He again waited for a few seconds and then said, "If the things are clear to you, we may start talking business."

Shiv Prasad did not say a word. He had guessed where the person stood. In fact he was slowly walking side to side along his table, a little away from him, closer to the wall. There was no point in making an effort to spring upon him. He will easily move sideways making him fall and hurt himself. There were no red lights in his room, which could be switched on. Even if there were, the guy won't give him an opportunity to switch off other lights and switch on the red ones. He glanced at the glass paper weights lying on his table. In a swift move these could be thrown on him. At least this will make him react. His gun might fall or he might get hurt. He began trying to figure when his attention might be slightly slack. He must buy time. The more time he had, the greater the possibility of overpowering him.

Elizabeth suddenly stopped her sobs and began listening to the sounds coming from Shiv Prasad's cabin. It was not Shiv Prasad's voice. Someone else was giving a kind of speech. Who might have entered his room without her knowledge? Curiosity took the better of her and she tiptoed to his room and began peeping from the narrow gap between the curtain and the door. Shiv Prasad sat with both hands raised above his head. Someone standing in front of him was speaking. She could not see any one there. And then she understood everything and felt the chill running through her. She ran back to call the attendants on duty. Her movement also attracted the attention of Aidni Rm.

This one fraction of a second was the moment Shiv Prasad had been waiting for. With lightening speed he picked up one of the paperweights and threw in the direction of sound. A loud "ouch" came from that direction. The paperweight bounced off before reaching the wall and fell, and with that also fell a revolver on the ground. Shiv Prasad pulled out the revolver from his drawer and fired in the same direction, but this time there was no sound of ouch, instead, the sound of someone running out of the room. The person running out had in the process pulled the curtain too strongly and it came down along with the pelmet. Shiv Prasad struggled through this curtain and pelmet and ran out following the sound, and shouting, "catch him, catch him" but the man had run quite ahead. The constables who had been alerted by Elizabeth, were running in the opposite direction, towards Shiv Prasad's cabin. But the man took them by surprise and pushing and hitting them, made his escape.

....

Ankit had resigned to his fate. He had been passing his days in the lock up without any information on when, if at all, he will be released or whether a case would be initiated against him. Doctors had examined him and had confirmed that he was mildly schizophrenic and had been programmed by some professional into carrying out the shooting. But the case had yet to be heard in a court of law.

Seeing Shiv Prasad and Elizabeth, he thought that he was about to be released. Shiv Prasad began asking him details of all that had happened before he began hearing his inner voice. His memory was sharp, but he used to miss facts in between. The statements sometimes did not correlate. Shiv Prasad had to ask the same questions in different ways and getting into minor and irrelevant details, in order to elicit correct information.

Elizabeth was recording all the statements. After about four hours of interrogation, Shiv Prasad concluded that he had all the information he could have from Ankit.

They sat down to analyze the information and decided to go to the house where Ankit had taken that foreigner couple. Both were confident that the foreigners were on the lookout for drugs and the person could provide a link to Aidni Rm.

They donned a wig and a hippy appearance, took Ankit with a small team of police constables to the house where Ankit had taken the foreigners. Leaving Ankit and the team a few blocks away, they walked to the house and knocked. A middle aged man came out and asked them what they wanted. Shiv Prasad said he wanted to see Duke. The man grew suspicious. "Who are you? Who told you about Duke? What do you want from him?"

His discomfort revealed a lot of things.

Shiv Prasad said, "One of our friends who has come from Russia and is living in Pahargunj, gave me his name and address." He paused and added, "He wanted something, but could not come. He has given me Dollars to pay for it."

The man thought for a while then said, "I don't know any Duke. You go and send your friend."

He turned to get back in to the house when Shiv Prasad pounced upon him and caught hold of his neck. Elizabeth picked up a whistle from the chain hanging round her neck and blew it. The police team arrived in a few seconds, even before the man could understand what was happening. He was handcuffed and they went inside the house. It was a single room tenement with a bed, a table, two chairs and several empty bottles of liquor and beer. The drawer in the table had three mobile phones. There was nothing which could be considered illegal or could justify a police raid like this. Shiv Prasad was aware that this matter could be blown out of proportion and used against him. However, he was used to taking such risks. They seized the phones and began asking him about Duke. The man kept denying any knowledge of Duke. Finally they took him to the police station.

Two of the mobile phones were like normal phones with several numbers and calls to and from. The third one interested Shiv Prasad and Elizabeth more. It had only one number in its contact list and all calls were made to or received from this one number. Shiv Prasad tried calling the number, but the number was switched off.

He read the messages, again only from and to the same number. The messages were mostly "call at… hrs". In the past week two messages had been sent to this number, saying, "supply needed. Call soon."

Elizabeth got the respondent number checked and for the first time they struck better luck. There were about a dozen callers for that number. They could not get the location from where all calls were made. It kept on changing. But they thought they were now able to see the faint suggestion of light at the end of the tunnel. Elizabeth issued instructions for tapping of all calls and messages from or to these numbers.

27

Rocky was walking in the Lodhi Gardens. It was evening and cold. There was hardly anybody around. Today's incident at the police office had unnerved him further. He was now sure that the police would now be even more alert. Probably there would be red lights all around. He had to be more alert and quickly do something about it. He had to continue his other running businesses through other accomplices. He will have to assign them more jobs and watch how they perform. The days were certainly not good but the show must go on, he thought. He reached a dark corner of the garden and took out his mobile. "Dinesh, are you willing to take up a special assignment?" He asked.

"Yes, sure I am."

"Tomorrow at ten AM sharp you will find a person buying India Kings at the cigarette shop in the shopping arcade of Ashok Hotel. Meet him like he is your old pal. He will give you a packet. Take that and keep moving here and there. At exact twelve, go to Nehru Park. You will find a man in red checkered shirt. Ask him where is the UK High Commission. He will take you to show the way. On the way exchange your packet with his and return. Report to me at exactly one PM. OK?"

"Yes boss"

The line got disconnected.

Rocky made some more calls from the same place, then walked slowly to the India Habitat Centre for a drink and dinner. At ten minutes to eleven, he came out and again walked into Lodhi Gardens, at almost the same place. He took out the other mobile and called.

"You made us wait very long" Voice of Baadshaah crackled over the phone even before Rocky could get the first indication of call going through.

"Yes, I had several things to settle here." He said.

"Ala Kamaan wants you to settle his score first." Baadshaah said.

"I told you not to hurry. It will simply make things more difficult."

"Ala Kamaan doesn't care." Baadshaah said. "I told him everything you said. He is not pleased. He wants action."

"If he is going to be pleased with a small diwali cracker, then he should not have approached me." Rocky was sarcastic.

"No diwali crackers, and no jokes." Baadshaah's annoyance could not be more accentuated.

"We don't have two republic days in a year." Rocky said.

"Yes. And Ala Kamaan does not have the patience to wait for the next republic day."

"So, what do you want?"

"There is going to be a special Cabinet meeting on security matters next week. All ministers are bound to attend. Our intelligence says even Army chief will be there. You can get ready to welcome them when they come out after the meeting from the Parliament House. They will be closely following each other. You may start from one end and move to the other end and by the time the security begins to fathom what's happening, you should be far away."

Rocky was pleased with this information. It sounded very good. With every passing day his risk was growing. Had he been successful in killing Shiv Prasad today, there would have been plenty of time. But with that effort failed, he had to hurry up before they catch up with him. If this plan was to be implemented within a week, probably the police would not be fully geared to take any counter measures. But he must lie low now. No more efforts to eliminate any one. Better be in hiding for some time and let them break their head. Nevertheless, he will have to do a recce to plan finer details. The first major issue was the gun. The gun Baadshaah had arranged last time was in Pratap's house and in all probability had by now been confiscated by the police.

Without expressing his excitement, he said, "I will have to think and plan the whole thing. But the first thing I definitely need is the toy you gave me for last planned action."

"Where is the toy?"

"Lost." Rocky calmly said, "Thanks to the goof up by my failed assistant."

"One of the most difficult things." Baadshaah sighed, "Do you have another man to come and pick up again like the last time?"

"I am afraid, not." Rocky knew Baadshaah will be able to manage a new gun for him easily.

"OK, you plan other things and I will see what I can do about this toy." Baadshaah said.

"This is the last call on this number. You will get my new number soon." Rocky said and disconnected. After having talked such sensitive things, it was not wise to talk again on this number. He walked out, got into his car and drove home.

28

"Passport office could not identify the man as the picture was quite blurred. Immigration authorities have also not seen any one looking similar going out or coming in." Elizabeth announced, "But I gave them the photograph of this lady also and both of them have identified her."

Shiv Prasad looked at the girl's passport and travel details. She was returning from Rome. He still believed that this girl had nothing to do with Aidni Rm.

The guy they had arrested at Geeta Colony was a small time drug trafficker. But his role was limited to passing messages only. He himself had not been handling drugs. His partner who handled drugs was Duke. He had disappeared immediately after the arrest was made. The man knew nothing about how the activities were carried out. He used to get messages on his phone and would pass on to the other concerned operators through the other phone. Besides Duke, he had never met any other dealer. He had been meeting consumers from time to time. Overall, this arrest also did not prove much for Shiv Prasad. He was again back at square one.

"Well, any feedback from the phone companies?" He asked.

Elizabeth opened the feedback notes from the phone companies. Most of the phones had remitted a one line message to one number, saying "supply needed." There had been no other calls or messages. All the phones were in switched off mode.

Just then the attendant brought in a fax message. It was a message from a phone company. A message had been sent by the number to three of the phones. It was a cryptic one word, "4 pm".

"A very cleverly organized racket!" sighed Shiv Prasad. "The guy has already arranged the supplies and would be delivering it at 4 PM today at a predetermined place.

"Please ask the phone companies to carefully note the location of the mobiles when they are switched on. They will surely be getting switched on sometime today, before 4 PM!"

"The phone from where the message was sent, was somewhere at Connaught Place about an hour ago. They cannot give a more precise location."

"That means this man was at Connaught Place at about 9 AM. He would be arranging the supplies during the day and deliver by 4. Since we have no leads again, I find no harm in checking this lady out. It should be a simple job – we have her address."

The lady was doing her research at JNU on sixteenth century Renaissance art. She was a very simple girl living with her parents. All of them were shocked to find crime branch officials at their home.

Shiv Prasad asked her, "Who else had been travelling with you?"

"No one. I travelled alone."

"On your return this one person claimed that his passport and documents were with you. Did you not have his documents?" Shiv Prasad passed on the photograph of the person to her.

She looked shocked. "How can anyone say so? I was travelling alone all through and have never carried anybody's documents."

But then looking at the picture, she gave an impression of recognition. "I think I have seen this man. He sat next to me in the plane. I can tell because his jacket looks strange. He did not remove his jacket in the plane also. He was also behaving a little erratically."

Both Shiv Prasad and Elizabeth were elated.

"What do you mean by erratic behavior?" Shiv Prasad asked.

"He occupied his seat too late. Probably he had a seat elsewhere, but came on the seat next to mine after the doors were closed, finding it vacant. I was a little wary because I had made a special request at the check in counter to keep the seat next to mine vacant if possible. And they usually oblige if there are vacant seats." She continued, "He did not misbehave, but again before the plane could stop, he ran back to the toilets even though the airhostess kept announcing everyone to remain seated. After that I could not see him. Probably because of the rush in the aisle, he could not return. But he was not travelling with me. I do not know him and have never carried his documents."

"Does his picture look correct? Can you tell more about his features?"

"He was seated on my side, so I did not see his face clearly. I can recognize him only because of this jacket."

They returned to their office. "At least we know that he travelled to Rome." Was all Shiv Prasad said, ruefully.

29

Rocky was walking on the DND expressway with his mobile stuck to his ear. His car stood on the side of the road with bonnet open. It gave the appearance that something had gone wrong and he was calling assistance. There were no pedestrians on this road so the fear of being overheard did not exist.

"Go to Gurdaspur and meet Sher khan at milestone 437 on NH 1A at exactly 6 pm tomorrow. Do not reach there more than three minutes earlier and do not wait more than five minutes if he does not turn up." Baadshaah disconnected after giving this one line message. He did not bother to even confirm whether Rocky had heard the full message correctly.

Rocky went back to his car, checked under the bonnet while stealthily looking around for any sneakers. Finding none, he shut the bonnet and drove on.

30

"The phones were in different parts of the city. Vasant Vihar, Peetam Pura, Laxmi Nagar. We could pinpoint only one phone." Said Elizabeth with a dejected smile on her face.

"One we could pin point? And where was that?" Shiv Prasad was excited.

She returned her dejected smile, "Geeta Nagar Police Station! It was this drug dealer's phone that we confiscated."

"Well, that is not that disappointing, Liz!" Shiv Prasad said, "It means that one of the consignments could not be delivered. Let us mull over what could be the reaction of our friend now.

"The unfortunate part is that Duke is absconding. This man was only a messenger so all that he would have done is pass the message to Duke and Duke would have arranged to lift the consignment.

"Another door closed on our face.

"But then when this guy sees that one of his consignments remain undelivered, what he might do?" Shiv Prasad asked.

"That will very much depend on how the consignments are delivered." Elizabeth said. There must be a person carrying the consignment and waiting at a selected point for the recipient to come. From what we have seen and understood so far, the two persons won't be knowing each other. They might be having some code words or signals only.

"Now if one of them does not turn up, the delivery boy would just return and send a message, 'failed delivery' and the organizer would arrange for a substitute.

"I don't see any possibility of a breakthrough in this." Elizabeth concluded.

"One more thing is further disturbing," Elizabeth began again after a brief pause, "This guy has several assistants. So it is unlikely that he would be distributing these consignments himself. He is probably roaming around freely in the city either visible or invisible and passing instructions.

"At most he may be watching them carrying out the orders correctly."

"I am not so much concerned with his drug business. I am worried about his other plans. I don't think even he would be wasting much of his energy on this low value activity. He must be concentrating on the bigger plan. My immediate worry is how to see him during day light. I have a strong feeling he may hit during broad day light at some public function. The reason is simple – our red light formula is ineffective in broad day light."

Elizabeth hesitatingly said, "Sir, I am not sure if it will work, but shouldn't we try using red eye glasses for some of our security personnel on body guard duty of VVIPs?"

Shiv Prasad hugged Elizabeth in excitement and then quickly separated with an embarrassed look, "I am sorry, Liz, but from where do you get these bright ideas? I am sure this will work. What I don't understand is why this simple solution did not strike me?"

Elizabeth was joyed, embarrassed and sad, all at the same time. The sting deep inside her hurt her again. She did not say anything. The next hour they spent passing necessary messages to all VVIP security agencies.

31

Collection of AK47 was far more simpler than he had thought. He had barely parked on the side of the highway at the milestone 234 that a Sumo came along side. The man peeped out and asked in punjabi if he had a problem. He shook his head in denial, said that he was waiting for Sher Khan and walked to the side of the highway presumably to pee. The Sumo drove away without waiting. He returned and found a bag on the back seat. He lifted the back seat and shoved the bag under it. Then he drove on. After a few kilometers, he took a U-turn to come back on the other side of the highway returning to Delhi.

The plan he had chalked out now was flawless. His worry of getting exposed in red lights also had subsided. He had checked his magic wrist band. During day, due to bright light, red light itself remains invisible. He had gone out and focused laser beams and very strong red light torch on himself, but nothing was visible. This meant he could carry out his mission during day without any fear.

He had also carried out his recce. It was so easy to walk in through the main gate of the Parliament House. They had opened the gate to let a VIP car in. He was waiting in his invisible form near the gate and had entered behind the car. He had walked up to the gate through which all MPs came out. In the front so many media personnel stood waiting with their cameras to get the news from the VVIPs. After speaking briefly to the media personnel, the VVIPs got into their cars and left.

He was however not very satisfied with this place. The VVIPs came out one after another. That means once he had started shooting, the ones still inside the building won't come out. He could walk in while shooting but still the targets could get sufficient cover. He estimated he won't be able to kill more than five. This won't be sufficient. Ala Kamaan definitely expected many more casualties. After all they were paying a billion dollars. He thought about moving in and getting inside the central hall, where Cabinet meetings take place. It would be best to do this inside the hall. It would be worse than Jallianwala bagh. He walked up to the central hall without any hindrance. It would be a cakewalk, he had concluded.

This time he had planned more meticulously. He won't allow any stupid assistant to goof up this time. The concern on republic day was that the security is very strict. They check all cars and parking is at predetermined places. Then the spectators have to walk a long distance. It is terribly crowded and it would be impossible for him to walk without getting pushed by any one. It would have been impossible to reach the VVIP enclosure from any side. Thus he had planned to stay at the Meridien which was at walking distance. Getting AK47 into the hotel was again impossible. So he had asked Pratap to deliver it on the morning of 26th near hotel Meridien. He would have then simply walked with the gun to the VVIP enclosure from the road side and gunned all of them in few minutes. It wouldn't have been difficult to run away in the melee that would have followed. Once in the crowd, he would have simply slipped out the magic band from his wrist to look like the lakhs of other ordinary spectators. Alas, Pratap could not gather enough courage or perhaps his stupid 'soul' woke up at the wrong time. Yes, wrong time. That's why he is no longer alive!

But this time he will ask Shailaja to drive him to Vijay Chowk in the morning. Around eight in the morning there are not many visitors. He will just walk down to a tree, walk behind it and slip on the band. Then will walk to the Parliament house and wait for the VVIPs to start coming. He was fully geared to accomplish this high profile assignment.

Immersed in his thoughts and dreams of a billion dollars, he reached home. He left the gun inside the car as it was. He would take it out in the morning just before starting, hide it in his jacket and then ask Shailaja to drop him at Vijay Chowk.

32

It was drizzling since morning. It was not so cold today, but had become a little humid. Rocky was not deterred by the rains or humidity. Getting inside the Parliament house premises was really cake walk. He had entered by nine thirty. At first he thought of walking straight into the central hall and sitting there calmly, waiting for the targets to arrive and the meeting to begin. Then once the meeting had started, he would start shooting, allowing no one an escape. He was about to go in, but suddenly he realized his mistake. The rains had wetted his shoes, If he went in, his footprints would remain visible. He should not make an attempt to go in until there were sufficient foot prints on the ground so that his prints could get mixed up.

Secondly, staying inside for a long time would be exposing him to risk. Anyone could move in with a red light. There were exit signs all around in red colour. If anyone got suspicious, the whole plan would fail. Not only fail, it was certain that this time he would be caught and that meant end of … well … not the game ….. his life!

He stayed outside near the media personnel under a small shed they had created to get protection from rains. He was enjoying their talks. He wondered what they would be talking after a few hours. How they would be scrambling to take the picture of slain national leaders and how all the channels would be screaming at the top of their voices giving the widest live coverage of any such happening. And how excited would be Ala Kamaan. He thought he would go in after about half of the VVIPs had arrived.

33

Special Protection Group is used to getting weird orders. Many don't make sense. But security of the VVIPs under the prevailing terrorist ridden condition is more challenging than one can think of. Terrorists keep devising new techniques and keep finding loopholes in the security system. The security agencies are required to think of what and how the terrorist might be thinking and planning and then find a counter measure before the terrorist gets the opportunity to implement his plan. No wonder, the orders sometimes had to be weird. Often officers were given specific individual instructions, which others in the same group did not know. This too was necessary as they could never be sure if one of them had been weaned away by the enemies. India had seen its popular Prime Minister being shot down by her own security guards. It had seen its Prime Minister being blown by a human bomb. How could anyone take this security lightly.

Amar Sinh Rathore fully appreciated his responsibilities as a member of this elite force and religiously followed the instructions. He was sitting in the chamber of his boss getting a briefing about latest security measures. Amar Sinh thought this was most weird of all instructions he had ever got. He found it difficult to believe that someone could become invisible. Even more ridiculous was the argument that the invisible person could be seen through red eye glasses.

Nevertheless, he had learnt not to question the intelligence of his superiors and follow their instructions. Except for causing a little inconvenience, wearing red glasses was not expected to come in the way of security any way. So he was confident he would be able to carry out his normal duties perfectly, unhindered by the red glasses. He put them on and looked around. Then he joked, "Well, I can confidently say, this invisible man is not here!"

The boss also laughed.

Amar Sinh's duty was to begin after the cabinet meeting ended today. He had to accompany the Prime Minister for the next four hours. The Prime Minister had no other engagements scheduled. He would be only going out from the Parliament House to the South Block and will stay there until his duty was over. So the duty was really light today. Presently the meeting was to start in a few minutes. Some Ministers had already arrived. He thought he should also test the glasses in the day light, outside the office.

He walked out and looked around. Just as he arrived, the Prime Minister also arrived. With the Prime Minister some of his assistants also were walking in. He had come out of the air conditioned room of his boss. Outside was warmer. Due to increased humidity, dew formed on his glasses and his view became foggy. He took out his glasses to wipe them but was shocked.

He saw one of the assistants with the incoming Prime Minister disappear as he took out the glasses. Without cleaning the glasses, he put them back on his nose and the man appeared again. He was walking slightly behind the entourage of the Prime Minister. He wore a leather jacket which looked oversized.

The briefing given to him a few minutes earlier was too fresh for him to have settled down. The report was correct. This man could become invisible, had managed to come inside the Parliament house and join the entourage of the Prime Minister. Soon he may be shooting and India would be losing its third Prime Minister to terrorists.

He had no time to wait or think or to alert any one. He took out his gun and began shooting. Aim of a Special Protection Group Officer never fails. The man fell down. But the shooting created a furore. Amar Sinh found himself in the tight grip of several other Security Personnel.

It all went so swiftly that he also could not understand what was happening. Pointing at the fallen man he began shouting, don't catch me you fools, catch the killer there. But no one would listen. He was overpowered and was being pulled out to the security offices. The media personnel were busy shooting the unbelievable incident. Some reporters ran to face the camera and began giving live commentary on the goings on.

34

Bhure Lal's neighbours had almost no information about the owner or the occupants of his apartment. Typical of metro cities like Delhi. All they could find was that the owner was a Junior Engineer in PWD and was posted in Agra. He rarely visited this place. They could finally dig out his name and address, and proceeded to Agra to meet him. From the PWD office they found that he had gone to some construction site and would return to office after lunch.

Having nothing better to do, Elizabeth and Shiv Prasad walked into a restaurant and occupied a table which gave a clear view of the Taj. In the morning sun the Taj looked glorious. They were immersed in their own thoughts. Elizabeth was sadly thinking about Shahjehan and Mumtaj and her own life. She was contemplating resignation. For Shiv Prasad it was difficult to think anything except the case in hand. He was wondering what this Aidni Rm might be up to and what trap could be set for him. A television on the wall was showing a cricket match between India and Australia. None of them had much interest in cricket any way, but from time to time glanced at the screen.

Shiv Prasad was gloomy. He said, "Liz, I am somehow not able to forgive myself. This guy is extremely dangerous. My every nerve is screaming that something very very terrible is in the offing. And when I look at the actions I took, I realize that I did so many mistakes. I could have caught this person. But I missed. Not once, but twice. We missed out on many important leads. We literally gave this man a fresh life at least twice.

"We were saved on the Republic day not because we were alert, but because he failed. Feeling of nationalism rose in the heart of one of his accomplices. This may not happen every time.

"Now, I am afraid he might strike any time, and this time we may not be so lucky...

Just then the TV screen displayed in bold red letters, "BREAKING NEWS" and immediately thereafter the announcer began screaming, "Terrorists have struck again in Delhi. They entered the Parliament house and fired five shots on the Prime Minister. Luckily none of the bullets hit him. The terrorist has been overpowered by the security forces."

Both Shiv Prasad and Elizabeth shivered, they left their table and walked closer to the screen. Several other guests in the restaurant also left their seats and crowded in front of the TV. The channel soon started showing visuals with their correspondent screaming out details. They showed the Prime Minister moving into the Parliament Building with several other people. And then sounds of gunshots. A clip of several security persons at one place apparently overpowering the terrorist.

The correspondent was saying "The Prime Minister was just entering the Parliament building for a crucial cabinet meeting when a terrorist fired several shots at him. Luckily none of the bullets hit him. The security personnel present around this area quickly over powered the terrorist and have taken him inside the building for interrogation."

Then they began interviewing the cameramen who were present there. The camera man said, "Though we were present there, we had been concentrating on the Prime Minister. Suddenly the gun shots came from close to this building on the side. None of us could see exactly from where the bullets came, and before we could divert our attention, the security forces had surrounded the terrorist. So we have not been able to get a glimpse of the person."

Elizabeth and Shiv Prasad looked at each other. Picture was more clear to them than the cameramen who were physically present at the site. The invisible man had got inside the Parliament House compound just as Shiv Prasad was fearing and had fired at the Prime Minister. To make matters worse, the security personnel trying to pounce upon the invisible man had caught one of the security men. Aidni Rm had once again been successful in escaping in spite of the tightest security arrangements. Once again the saving grace was luck, and not the security arrangements. Only luckily none of his bullets had found its way into the body of the Prime Minister. Shiv Prasad felt ashamed of his failure.

They decided to cancel the program to meet this person and returned to Delhi. Shiv Prasad met the SPG officer who was arrested on the charge of attempt to assassinate the Prime Minister. He explained that he had seen this man through his red goggles and also found that without goggles he was invisible. This was exactly in line with the brief given to him just a few minutes before this shooting. However, no one was now buying his story. Shiv Prasad asked him whether he was sure that at least one of his bullets had hit the person. He said he was a sharp shooter and he was confident that at least three bullets must have hit him. Since he was immediately pounced upon by other security personnel, his last two shots could have missed him. He also said that as is usual, he had tried to hit the person on his lower body and so he was hit in the waist and legs only.

Shiv Prasad went to the gate where the invisible man was said to have been shot. There was nothing to be seen there. He moved away from there and a few feet away saw some drops of blood on the ground. He understood, the man must have run away this way after getting shot. He moved along the trail of blood. It went out of the parliament compound and then towards the lawns on the sides of Rajpath. At one place under a tree there was considerable blood. It was surprising why no one had noticed it. Probably because it was on the offside of the road, behind a tree. Aidni Rm must have rested and waited for a car here. Shiv Prasad thought. The blood trail ended here, and Shiv Prasad had once again no clue of where to move next.

35

Rocky was badly hurt. Several bullets had hit him like rain drops. His entire right side seemed to be burning and paralysed. He himself could not believe how he had managed to run from the site, out of the parliament house compound and all the way up to the lawns. Thanks to the panic and confusion which followed the shooting, the gate remained open for a few minutes, albeit with several police men on the gate. This gave him the opportunity to run out of the compound. Otherwise he would have been trapped in, and with these wounds would not have been able to move at all after some time. He had called Shailaja sitting under the tree and hoping that the road was not blocked as a consequence of this firing. Luckily, this side of the road was not blocked. The roads near the Parliament House had been sealed. He had lost a lot of blood and was cursing Delhi traffic which might be delaying Shailaja. But Shailaja came very fast. Hardly in ten minutes. He thought he was about to lose consciousness. His vision had blurred already. Still he could see his car slowly moving towards the tree. Shailaja was looking all around and apparently was not able to see him. He pulled the band out of his wrist, put it in his pocket and pressed the redial key on his mobile. Just then Shailaja saw him and brought the car close. He was scared stiff that some police man would see them but luckily no one did. He took a couple of minutes to get into the car, lied down on the back seat and began trying to tell Shailaja what to do.

"Shaila, I am very badly hurt. Several bullets have pierced into me. I may lose consciousness soon. You have to find a surgeon who would take these bullets out but keep his mouth shut. Don't try to save money. Just find the right doctor. It's life or death for us, Shaila." And he passed out.

Shailaja was completely at a loss. She was unable to think what to do. Alone she won't be able to take unconscious Rocky out of the car. Where to find help? And help was needed quickly. Her common sense told her that no doctor would operate and remove the bullets without informing the police. Prima facie, it was a case of attempt to murder. In fact people may think that she herself had been trying to murder him. Driving him in the car like this was also very risky. In Delhi there is always a lot of checking on the streets. At any point someone might check their car and the whole story would end there.

Suddenly as a blessing she recalled her cousin who had studied medical in Ukraine only to find that his degree was not recognized in India and so was unable to either get a job or start his own practice. He lived a miserable life somewhere in the outskirts of Delhi, probably working in some call centre. She had never bothered to call him leave alone meet him. But today he seemed to be the only possible savior. She did not have his address or phone number. She called one of her friends who might be having his phone number. She was in luck. She called him and said without trying to hide the panic, "Rahul, I am in a very serious problem and I need your urgent help. Do you have your medical implements?"

He laughed sadly, "Shaila, what is the use? I am not authorized to use them!"

"I still need your help. Please pick up all your implements, tools and whatever you have, related to medical, and tell me how fast you can meet me and where?"

"What's the matter, Shaila?" He was perplexed.

"Can't tell now. You just tell me where should I meet you. It is urgent."

Rahul guessed Shailaja wanted to get some illegal abortion done. He knew that she was living with some boy friend without marriage. But getting an abortion done is simple in Delhi. A person with Shailaja's kind of resources did not need Rahul's help. Nevertheless, He could not refuse the one opportunity which was coming his way after three years of getting a medical degree. To get assured, he said, "Shaila, I am not a gynecologist by the way."

Shailaja impatiently retorted, "It has nothing to do with gynecology. Tell me where should I meet you Rahul, I have very little time."

After about twenty minutes Shailaja picked up Rahul from a colony in East Delhi and sped towards Golf links. Rahul sitting on the passenger seat in the front looked back at Rocky, felt his pulse and under the eyelids. He looked grim. "Shaila, I do not know what has brought him to this condition, but let me tell you, he is pretty serious and needs professional medical help. He has probably bled too much. His pulse is almost dead. He must be transfused blood urgently. My sincere suggestion is you do not take any chances and rush towards the nearest hospital or private nursing home."

Shailaja retorted, "Taking him any where is out of question. That's why I sought your help. Please tell me all that you may need. I will get that and you have to treat him at our home. Any thing you need to buy, please tell, don't worry about the cost."

"It's not a question of cost, Shaila. He needs fresh blood. You can't buy that. Even if you are able to find a donor, we need to test the blood first in a pathological laboratory. I can't do that test. Any treatment can begin after his pulse becomes a little regular. By the way, what happened to him?"

Shailaja got busy making a phone call. "Bahadur, Sahab has been hurt badly. I am bringing him home. Please be ready with Rajender and Shamu to take him out of the car and into the bed room quickly. He will need a stretcher. You may bring any charpoy or small bed to use as stretcher."

"......."

"No, no, no need to call a doctor. The doctor is with me. Please do not let anyone know that he is injured. It will be bad for our business. This information must not be leaked out of our home. Tell everyone seriously. And yes, As soon as we reach, I will give you a list of medicines to be brought quickly. Please tell Shamu to be ready."

She turned to Rahul, "please quickly write down all the medicines, implements you may need. Including scalpel or anesthetics. I will get them in a few minutes."

"You did not tell me what has happened to him. Was it a road accident?"

"I will tell you in detail when we reach home. You may please concentrate on the list."

Rahul wanted to say something, but preferred to remain silent and began scribbling on a note pad.

As soon as they reached the gate, it opened. Without stopping Shailaja drove to the porch. A Nepalese watchman and two more servants were ready with a charpoy. They opened the car door and began lifting Rocky. He was laid in the charpoy and the charpoy was quickly moved to the bedroom. Shailaja and Rahul followed into the bed room. Rocky was then transferred to their bed and the servants took the charpoy out. Rocky's trouser was drenched in blood. Shailaja handed over the slip from Rahul to one of the servants, directed him to get all the medicines quickly, closed the door behind them and began removing the jacket. As soon as she unbuttoned the jacket, an AK47 came out. Not only Rahul, Shailaja herself was also shocked. She had not even imagined that Rocky could have been involved in such deadly things. Rahul asked, "Shailaja, what is this? What are you guys upto? I can help you in some things, but I definitely can't be helping a terrorist. I am afraid, I will have to inform the police."

"Wait, Rahul. You do not know what exactly has happened, what had he been doing. Even I do not know. Please have some patience. Let him first get well, then you ask him what he had been doing. Do not act on impulse."

"Look, Shailaja! Whatever he had been doing, having an AK47 itself is a crime. He is definitely not serving in any of the security forces. So he is a criminal and a serious criminal at that, with deadly intentions. I don't think we need to know what exactly he had been doing. The police may be more interested in that. I am sorry, Shailaja, I am leaving now and would be going straight to the police station. I cannot be a party to any such crime."

"Rahul, I again say, as a doctor, and as a human being, your first responsibility is to save his life. Please do that first. We shall talk about other things later." She had by this time not only removed his jacket, but also trousers and brief, making him completely naked below waist. He had three bullet wounds. Two in hip, one in thigh. The wounds were covered with thick clot of blood. Bleeding had stopped some time ago due to these clots. There were no other injuries any where below the waist. Rahul began cleaning up his wounds and Shailaja began removing his shirt. There was no blood on the shirt. There were no injuries also on the upper part of the body. But a couple of bullets had fallen from the jacket. She was wondering where had the bullets come from or where had they hit him. Rahul understood her anxiety and offered an explanation, "Probably these bullets hit the rifle he was carrying and so he has not been hurt."

The explanation sounded logical.

The servant brought the medicines and the implements. Shailaja crack opened the door and took them. Rahul now sat down to clean the wounds with spirit. As soon as the dried clot was cleared, blood began oozing out. He covered it with cotton and then took out tweezers. "Lucky that he is unconscious. I don't have any anesthetics. This is going to be a very painful operation."

The bullet came out in no time but with it suddenly blood also began gushing out. He covered it with cotton again and kept it pressed hard against the wound. Same operation was carried out thrice to take out all the three bullets. He shaved the area around the wounds, pressed each of the wound with thick pad of cotton and stuck it with wide adhesive tapes. He took the pulse again and gave Shailaja a worried look. Shailaja brought a pyjama and slipped it on him taking utmost care not to hurt. Rahul unsealed a glucose bottle and inserted a needle into the rubber stopper. He inserted a needle into a vein on the back of Rocky's palm and affixed with adhesive tapes. Shailaja hung the glucose bottle from a nail in the wall. He regulated the flow of glucose and then appeared to be slightly relaxed.

"Shailaja, He actually should be given blood. We have no way to arrange and transfuse blood. I don't know how long will he take this way. The only good thing is that he is strong and in good health otherwise. Now we have to wait for him to slowly recover and gain consciousness. Once he starts taking food, we can expect better recovery."

"I am sure he will recover fast." Shailaja said.

"Now, Shailaja, once again I tell you, my conscious does not allow me to remain silent. I am convinced that he had been involved in some terrorist activity and won't be surprised to know that he was shot by the police. Assisting him is also a criminal act. I have any way extended all help that I could. I think I should go now."

"What consciousness you are talking about, Rahul? What has your conscious given you so far? A degree with no value? Your dad spent several lakhs of rupees, and you spent a good seven years studying medicine in a far off strange country braving freezing temperatures eating insipid food and living a miserable life to finally end up in a call center earning ten thousand bucks a month? You can never find a suitable job in India or anywhere in Europe. Ukraine would not accept you. You can't even start your own practice. What is your conscious going to give you in the remaining life of yours? Not even a useless brass medal. You are probably not going to be able to live even an average life. Why don't you understand and leave your conscious out for some time? I will pay you rupees one lakh per day for the next fifteen days. But you have to keep your mouth shut. Keep your conscious silent. Just imagine. Fifteen lakh rupees in fifteen days. And no one is ever going to find out about all this. My servants are very loyal to me. After fifteen days he will be ok and you will be free. Just for a short while, earn for yourself. You may perhaps never get a similar opportunity."

Rahul was still not convinced but he understood the meaning of fifteen lakh rupees. It was indeed something which he could not resist. Not in his present position. He remained silent, weighing his options. Shailaja was looking intently at him, commending herself for her persuasive little speech.

"What are you going to tell the servants?"

"That he met with a road accident. But since the accident was inadvertently caused by one of his friends, we do not want the police to be informed. The servants are anyway not very inquisitive. I don't think they will probe more or even talk about it outside. You are seeing our house – we don't have any prying neighbours also. So you should not worry about it at all."

Rahul did not say anything. Fifteen lakh was a big amount. After a while he said again, "I think I should go now. I will come back tomorrow. He should be feeling better and probably gain consciousness also by then. Luckily the bullets were only in the hips and thighs. He may probably take some time to start walking, and may even walk with a little limp. But his life is not in danger."

"Rahul, please stay back. I can't go to any other doctor. If he needs any help in the night, I will be in a very bad position."

Rahul silently agreed. Fifteen lakh was a big amount!

....

Rocky gained consciousness much faster than they had thought. He began moving his limbs and moaning by midnight. Rahul added some more medicines in the glucose bottle through a syringe and looked more relaxed. Rocky got up in the morning appearing to be in very good shape. Because of the wounds in the hip and thigh he was not able to sit or stand, but otherwise he seemed to be perfectly OK. He expressed his desire to have a cup of tea. Rahul removed the glucose drip and Shailaja asked her servants to get tea and some biscuits. They arranged several pillows to support his back and he sat in a reclining position. He looked questioningly at Rahul. Shailaja introduced him as her cousin with a medical education, and that he was the reason behind his fast recovery. Rocky smiled gratefully. "How long do you think it will take to heal?"

"Not less than fifteen days." Rahul said, "Being in hips and thighs, you will have problem walking. But otherwise you should be ok by tomorrow. And you should not put load on your legs, as it may delay healing."

"May I know how this happened?" Rahul asked.

Rocky appeared disturbed. This was one question he did not want asked. Even by Shailaja. He did not want to answer it. He remained silent. Rahul did not repeat the question.

The servant brought in the news papers. The thick headline screamed about the attack on the Prime Minister. Rahul saw it and appeared far more frightened than at the sight of AK47 the previous night. He looked wide eyed at Rocky. The question was writ large on his face – does your wound have anything to do with this? Shailaja too had seen the headline and had the same look on her face. Both Shailaja and Rahul were petrified. A stunned silence followed. Rocky did not say a word. He calmly took the news paper and began reading it, pretending to be oblivious of their strong reaction. But as he read it, he himself got perplexed. He had probably acted as a shield to the Prime Minister, saving him from the bullets of an assassin. The assassin was one of the security officers of the elite SPG! Had he not been there, it would have been a repeated history. Another Prime Minister killed by his own security men! What a strange coincidence! One could-have-been assassin inadvertently protected his target from another assassin! Now he could build stories around this incidence. Of course different stories - one for his sponsors and another for his girl friend and others. His game had not ended yet. His fear of yesterday was unfounded. He could still carry out his plans. And to his sponsors he could tell that his effort failed once again, but the effort was indeed made! Well! The story could be woven around the actual happenings. He was overjoyed.

He looked up from the news paper. Both Shailaja and Rahul were still gazing him. "What? Why are you looking at me like that?"

They both exchanged glances. Rahul asked, "Does this news have any connection with you? There had been a serious attack on the Prime Minister. He escaped unhurt but you had five bullets. Three hit you and two missed you. And you had been carrying an AK47. No ordinary person can have an AK47. Please tell the truth, what has actually happened."

"I am sorry, I am not supposed to reveal anything. I was on some very serious assignment. I can't tell you everything, but yes, you are right to guess - I have some connection with this news. Is it important for you?"

"Look Rocky, you have been involved in a very serious terror attack on the Prime Minister. You must be the most wanted terrorist today. In your company, we too run the risk of being labeled terrorists. I am afraid I will have to inform the police."

Rocky laughed, "So you think I was the one who attacked? You think that I fired the gun at the Prime Minister, but the barrel pointed on my back! How funny! And then why did they leave me and arrest some other innocent person?"

"Of course you did not fire. But you yourself said that this news has some connection with you. What else can we think?"

"Think logically dear! The attacker has been arrested. There were bullets fired. Those bullets did not enter the body of the Prime Minister- the intended target- but me. Where does that put me? A killer or a savior?"

"But why did you not want to go to a hospital? Why this secrecy? Why get the treatment from an unauthorized person and risk your life? If you were indeed the savior, you would have been now receiving the awards and accolades."

"That's what I said, can't be revealed. You have heard the story of Sarabjit Singh, who has been languishing in Pakistani jails, facing execution? Why? The answer can only be guessed by the people. The fact cannot be accepted by anyone, even those who know it very well."

Rahul kept looking at him unbelievingly. "You mean you are an undercover security officer attached to the Prime Minister? Why should the Prime Minister be having an undercover security officer within his own country when he is having such a large posse of real security men?"

"This is not for me to answer. These things are decided at very high levels and they only know the answers. We at lower levels just execute the orders."

"And from that low level you have such income that you live in this lavish bungalow at Golf Links and move around in swanky cars?

"Of course not. The job is only for my personal satisfaction. I have inherited enough and don't need to work for a living. I want to do something for the country. I want some adventure in my life. That's just it. If you don't believe, you may go and inform the police. While nothing can be established against me simply because I have done nothing wrong, it may be very difficult for me to explain what I have been doing and where I got the gun from, because an undercover spy or a security agent does not create alibis to prove his innocence. You may inform the police if you like, but it will be against national interest. The decision is yours."

Rahul couldn't decide whether to believe him or not. His explanation did not sound too convincing, but he did not have much idea of how VIP security works. He stood there for some time looking at the floor and then said, "OK, Shailaja, now that he is in a much better condition, may I go and have some rest?"

"Sure. The next door on the left side is your bed room. Please do not hesitate to call the servants if you need anything anytime. I suggest you stay with us for some more days –till his wounds heal."

Rahul nodded and left. As soon as he was out, Shailaja looked straight into the eyes of Rocky and said, "That was a wonderful story, Rocky! But it was good only for Rahul. Don't expect me to believe any of it. I know you won't like to share the truth with me, but let me tell you, the support you can get from me, won't come from anyone else."

"No, I won't hide from you, Shaila!" Rocky had realized that for moving any further, a dependable accomplice was imperative. The next couple of hours was spent in explaining the incidents, the working of the magic wrist band and the future plans. Since the attack on the Prime Minister had failed, and next such opportunity may not be so close, the highest priority was now eliminating Shiv Prasad. Rocky told Shailaja that he was a very dangerous police officer of crime branch and could foil all his plans. In fact when he got fired at the Parliament House, he was thinking that Shiv Prasad had found him out even during day light. It was only through the news paper reports that he realized that another security officer had been on the prowl.

36

"Look, madam! I am his secretary, and I am supposed to know who wants to meet him and why. There is hardly anything he keeps from me. So you need not be so secretive. Please tell me what do you want to discuss with him." Elizabeth argued.

The beautiful mod girl was not willing to share either her identity or the topic of her intended discussion with Shiv Prasad. Finally Elizabeth gave up. She asked Shiv Prasad on the intercom and allowed her to go in. But then asked to check her bag for security reasons. She objected saying that the bag had already been checked at the entry by the security officers. Elizabeth politely apologized, and cited the rules. She passed her bag to Elizabeth. She looked in, groped the objects in the bag and then returned it. She went into the cabin of Shiv Prasad.

"Sir," the girl addressed Shiv Prasad in a hushed tone, "I am afraid my boy friend is involved in some terrorist activities. He was badly wounded in some gun attack. He asked me not to inform the police and get him treated through some private doctor. Then I saw the news about the attack on the Prime Minister. I am scared. I do not know what to do. If he comes to know, he may kill me. Luckily now he is bed ridden so I gathered courage to come up to you."

Shiv Prasad kept getting details from her for about half an hour and then decided to go along with her to the place where he was hiding and arrest him. The girl did not want him to take several police men along to avoid bad publicity for herself and also to avoid getting him alerted.

On his way out Shiv Prasad peeped into Elizabeth's cabin and told her that he was going out with Shailaja. He could sense a hint of worry on Elizabeth's face. She probably wanted to tell something. Shiv Prasad pondered for a moment. Elizabeth said, "Could you wait for a moment so that the driver could be ready?"

"Shailaja says she will drive me there." Elizabeth's look was sending him warning signals. He added, "But I think you may tell the driver to follow me so she will not have to drop me back here at the office."

Shiv Prasad wanted to speak to Elizabeth privately to understand her concerns but Shailaja's presence would not make it possible. He decided to give her a couple of minutes to organize the car and driver or any other measures she wanted to take. He slowly walked down and out of the office. Just out side the office he again stopped to talk to another police officer and then moved towards Shailaja's car which was a few meters away. While sitting in the car he looked back to see the police jeep ready to follow him with the driver waiting outside looking towards him for any last minute instructions. Then he noticed a slight movement on the left side of the jeep as if someone had sat on the passenger side. But there was no one in sight. All his senses came to full attention. He could guess why Elizabeth looked worried. He again paused for a few moments thinking whether to jump and catch hold of Aidni Rm, who had just now sat inside the jeep or go further with Shailaja, to get to the root. It would certainly be pretty easy to catch and arrest Aidni Rm here. He was sitting in the jeep, and may not be able to run out quickly enough.

He felt stupid having left his red goggles in his office, even though he knew that he was going to encounter Aidni Rm. By going with Shailaja he was simply walking into the trap laid by them. Another option was to shoot him. He was certainly sitting in the passenger seat in the jeep and would surely be shot. But he also wanted to find something more about this gang. So far they knew nothing. His instincts were failing him. Something was stopping him from either firing or jumping and catching the wanted criminal who was now within his easy reach. Shailaja was sitting on the driving seat and looking at him questioningly. He did not waste any more time and sat down in the car. The car quickly moved and he heard the jeep also following him. He was wondering what these people intended to do now. In all probability they may take him to some deserted house and kill him there. Because his earlier effort to kill him in the office had failed. The security in the office had been strengthened and several red lights had been installed at different places. That had probably deterred Aidni Rm from entering his office to make a second attempt at his life. But now he had identified an accomplice. The CCTV at the office would certainly have captured some of her images.

The car was now running on Sardar Patel Marg. On the right side was the ridge, called the lungs of Delhi. The car stopped at a place where there were no buildings around. The right side of the road was full of wild bushes and trees. Shiv Prasad wondered what was this lady up to. The locale appeared to be the best suited for murdering someone and leaving the body for vultures and jackals. He said, "I thought you were taking me to a house where Aidni Rm is bed ridden."

"That's right." She said, "You don't expect a terrorist to be living in a densely populated colony. He is here in a small hut, away from every one's sight."

She jumped over the iron railing and began walking into the jungles. Shiv Prasad followed her. The ground was slightly wet and slippery. Also the jungles were a little higher than the road so they had to climb up. Shiv Prasad's ears were carefully recording every noise behind them, to trace the movements of Aidni Rm. He won't fire here, so close to the road, but he needed to be in readiness to counter any moves by him. He did get some indications of a person walking carefully behind him. They walked about a couple of hundred meters inside the jungles. Then again there was a little mound where they had to walk uphill. Shiv Prasad was now getting a feel that the place had become suitable enough for Aidni Rm to shoot him, and he may come in action any moment. He had focused all his senses on the invisible moving person behind him. But except for the sound of walking, no other motions could be sensed. But suddenly Shailaja slipped and fell. He had not expected this and on an impulse tried to hold and support her. But she fell. Even now he was more concerned about the activities from his behind. Aidni Rm would sure be taking the advantage of this incidence. But there was no movement. Aidni Rm had also stopped. Then he saw a revolver in Shailaja's hand. She was lying on the wet ground on her back holding the gun pointed towards him. He found his own revolver was missing. Shailaja had very smartly pretended to be falling and had grabbed his revolver while he was trying to support her. He cursed himself for concentrating solely on Aidni Rm and almost ignoring Shailaja. He had not expected this frail looking girl to be so smart. But even now he was not worried much about her. The bigger fear was still from Aidni Rm, who in his invisible form was in a much better position to attack him. He was concentrating on all sounds from all around to trace the position of Aidni Rm. Then a small branch lying in the ground tweaked and gave away his location. He was a little away. Probably waiting for the most opportune moment. But why not now? He certainly was in a commanding position now. Shiv Prasad decided not to waste any more time. With a swift movement of his right foot, he kicked Shailaja's hand holding the gun. The gun flew up and disappeared in the bushes behind. Shailaja screamed with pain and caught her right palm with the left. In the same breath, Shiv Prasad too fell down and caught Shailaja tight to use her as shield in case of any attack by Aidni Rm. But surprisingly, Aidni RM made no efforts to overpower Shiv Prasad or shoot him. He instead leapt in the direction where the gun had gone. Shiv Prasad got the exact location of where he was and leaving Shailaja, leapt to grab him. He had no time to think why Aidni Rm was playing this odd game of cat and mouse. Why he had been leaving all good opportunities of killing him. Shailaja too did not waste a moment and sprang up and bolted away from him.

In a moment he had jumped exactly upon Aidni Rm and grabbed him. He held him very strongly circling his arms round his body including arms. He also entangled his legs with his own, so he could not easily free himself and run. Shiv Prasad had missed him several times and was very well aware that he could somehow manage to get free and run away again. He did not want to miss this opportunity again. Further, this time he and his girl friend were bent upon killing him, fully planned and well prepared. But he was surprised to hear a feminine scream from him. The feel was also feminine. It was not Aidni Rm but another female accomplice of him. They both fell on the ground, but Shiv Prasad did not loosen his grip.

"It's me sir." The feminine voice came from the invisible person.

"You? How come?" He was shocked to hear Elizabeth.

The next moment she became visible with the magic band in her right hand.

"I don't understand. What is happening? How did you get this? What are you doing with these terrorists?" Shiv Prasad was perplexed. They were still sitting in the same position – Shiv Prasad practically had her completely in his lap, holding her strongly like a captured terrorist who could give him a slip any time.

And then suddenly appeared Shailaja again, with a gun in her hand, pointing at them.

"You will sure not understand. And there is no need for you to understand either. Because in a few minutes you both will be dead. After death you may keep talking endlessly and understand all secrets at leisure." Shailaja said, "Now, you bitch! Throw that magic band back to me, which you had stolen from my bag on the pretext of searching it."

Elizabeth turned her head to look at Shiv Prasad. He was still trying to understand. Shailaja was standing quite away. There was no way he could pound on her. In any case Elizabeth was almost sitting in his lap. Before he could jump, he would have to move Elizabeth from his lap. He looked around. There was nothing which could be thrown at her either. So the trick he played on Aidni Rm in his office could not be played again.

"Come on bitch. Quick. Throw it back to me." Shailaja shouted.

Shiv Prasad took the magic band from Elizabeth. With his fingers he spread it, trying to break it. But it was very elastic. It spread easily to the extent he could expand his fingers. Shailaja saw it and warned, "You try to do anything to that band and your life would be shortened further."

He made a gesture of throwing it at Shailaja, but in a quick move he slipped it on both his and Elizabeth's left wrists, Spread his legs holding Elizabeth's tight between them, lied down pulling Elizabeth tightly embraced with himself and rolled quickly to a side. Aghast, with the gun in her hand, Shailaja kept gazing at the place where Elizabeth and Shiv Prasad had been sitting a moment ago. She then fired in that direction. Shiv Prasad and Elizabeth were a few feet away from where the bullets hit the ground. Shiv Prasad was still holding Elizabeth in his strong grip. His wrist tied to Elizabeth's through the magic band, clasping her whole body in his own, making them look like one single body, as he feared that if they got separated the magic band may become ineffective. Or at least may make part of their bodies visible. They both lay silently. There was nothing Shiv Kumar could do now except wait. Shailaja was still away and could not be over powered in one swift action. Separating from Elizabeth could give them away. But holding that magnificent young body completely entertwined with his own was having some other effect on him. The sweet mild fragrance of her perfume was making him restless. Her soft body in his tight grip, every part of her body in direct contact with his own was the kind of experience he never had. Her softness was turning his own soft part getting into an embarrassing hardness. He was surprised how it could be happening when the fear of death was right in front of their eyes. Does the brain not control sexual desires? He began taking deep breaths.

Yoga could probably help, but it seemed to have no effect on him. At least now. He was finding it difficult to continue holding Elizabeth. Was Elizabeth getting any feel of his embarrassing situation? If she was, how on earth will he ever face her? Moving away from her immediately was becoming imperative, but that carried serious risk to both their lives.

The masculine grip of Shiv Prasad and the warmth it transmitted, was having a similar effect on Elizabeth. She had always been a very reserved type of girl with whom the boys never dared to make advances. No boy had ever touched her except for the occasional hand shakes. And today she was lying in a tight embrace of a person whom she …..well….. she…. admired…… in her heart. She recalled the day when they were sitting opposite to each other at the restaurant on the mountain top. The feelings and thoughts that she was having then. But she also knew in her heart that her thoughts may never become a reality. Even today it was just the circumstances which had led to this situation. But somehow the gravity of the situation did not seem to be overpowering her. The open jungle, wet, slightly muddy ground and a gun on the lookout of their heads – nothing seemed to exist…. what existed was a heavenly warm, tight embrace. She was feeling very comfortable and safe, and in absolute bliss. She seemed to be longing for it to continue endlessly.

Shailaja fired one more round a little away from the previous target. This bullet was closer to them but still did not touch either of them. Shiv Prasad forced himself to think about death standing a few feet from him, but he had never been scared of death and today when he wanted this fear to grip him just to save him from the situation which he felt was worse than death itself, it did not seem to have any intention of coming any closer to him! They remained motionless, with Shiv Prasad continuing his futile deep breathing exercises. Suddenly, to his great relief, Shailaja turned and began running away towards the street. Shiv Prasad did not lose a moment. He released his wrist from the band, pushed Elizabeth away, and began getting up passing quick instructions to Elizabeth, "quickly find the gun and stay here. I am going to catch her." His hardness was slowly turning soft again. Elizabeth also began returning to reality.

He ran out but could not see her. She must have run to the car and will try to drive away. He thought and kept running towards the street. On the street both her car and his jeep stood still, with no sight of her. Thinking that she must be hiding somewhere in the jungles only, he turned back and heard a gun shot. He ran towards where he had left Elizabeth. Elizabeth stood there holding her hand. His gun was lying on the ground. Shailaja was not to be seen anywhere. But he heard footsteps running away. He followed them. She had apparently put the band on her wrist and was quite ahead, running towards the street. He followed only to find the door of her car open and close and the car speeding away. He watched her driving away helplessly. There was no way he could pass instructions to the driver either. The driver wouldn't have been able to chase her on his own.

He returned to help Elizabeth. The bullet had pierced her palm and it was bleeding badly. She was in deep pain but more than physical pain from the bullet, the pain of having failed, the pain of having lost the magic band, and most of all the pain of missing the opportunity of catching the dreaded terrorist was hurting her. Shiv Prasad tried to stop the bleeding with his handkerchief and comforting her, took her to the police jeep waiting on the street. The driver was still looking wide eyed at where the car stood a few minutes ago. He blurted, "Sir, no one came. The car door opened and closed itself and the car went away on its own!" He had as yet not expressed his surprise at how Elizabeth had suddenly appeared in the scene!

Shiv Prasad asked him to drive to the nearest hospital. On the way, he asked Elizabeth what all had happened. She said, "I had found the gun and was picking it up when suddenly the bullet hit me in the hand. I saw Shailaja standing very close. She just snatched the magic band from me, put it on her own wrist and began running. You came almost immediately, but she had already disappeared and had been running."

"How did you get the magic band from her in the first place?"

"She wanted to meet you and was not telling me either her identity or the purpose. Just to be cautious, I asked to check her bag before allowing her in your office. In the bag I found this magic band. You remember, Mr. Anil had given such a good description of it, I immediately recognized it, and stealthily removed it from her bag. The thoughts of ethics or morals did not strike me at all! Once she was away, I tried it on and my suspicion got confirmed. I disappeared immediately from my own view. This was the magic band. The lady had come to kill you. I was still not worried much because I knew that if she remained visible, she won't be able to harm you. When you wanted to go out, then also I was not worried because I knew that without the magic band she won't be able to get invisible and so won't be able to harm you. In fact it would give you an added advantage because whatever plan she had made, would fail at the most crucial moment when she would need the magic band and find it missing. Still, I wanted to tell you about this and also to be around you for help, when you need it. So I decided to follow you like Mr. India!" She laughed, and then shivered at the thought of those few moments in the jungle.

Shiv Prasad was considering all possibilities. Elizabeth spoke again, "But all these days I had been thinking that Aidni Rm was a male. She should have at least changed her name to Mrs. India or Aidni Srm!" She laughed again.

"She is not Aidni Rm" Shiv Prasad said. "She is an accomplice of Aidni Rm. We had seen the outline on the footage from the airport. The built was masculine. She has a very feminine body. She was definitely not in the footage. We also heard his voice in my office. So now my worry is, whether they have two or more such gadgets? Or Aidni Rm passed his gadget to her to eliminate me? Then why he himself did not come? Is he hurt? Badly? Will he be back in business in a few days? And the most important of all, now is he going to concentrate on me or does he have any other more serious plans. The last planned attack on the Prime Minister failed. But unfortunately the higher authorities are still not seized of the danger posed by this terrorist. In fact they are not even believing this poor Amar Sinh Rathore who saved the Prime Minister and other Cabinet Ministers that day by firing on this invisible man. The proposal for red goggles is being taken by them as a ruse only for implementing the grandiose plan of assassinating the Prime Minister by Amar Sinh Rathore and his accomplices. After that one day, distribution of red goggles has taken a back seat. I don't know how long will they enquire and when will they start believing us. How can they be so casual on this aspect?"

Elizabeth too began thinking on these lines, while the car stopped at a hospital.

37

Rocky was lying on his bed and Shailaja sat near him, both glum faced.

"I don't know why I didn't shoot him as soon as I had the gun in my hand. That could have changed the scenario altogether." Shailaja said in a low voice.

"My reflexes worked well when he jumped to the bushes after that lady – I ran and brought my own gun from the car in less than a minute. But then again I did not shoot. In fact I had then only found that the bitch had stolen my magic band and my highest priority shifted to getting the band back." She continued.

"We lost another opportunity, but thanks to your wits, at least the magic band is back with us."

"This fact pains me even more – I had become invisible, I had the gun in my hand and this man was running behind me. I could have just stopped, turned and shot him. It would have been so easy. But I got panicked."

"I have more serious worries now. They have identified you. It should be easy for them to circulate your pictures and nab you. Worse still, they know the description and number of the car. This car can easily be stopped at any traffic junction. Luckily the address of the owner is given as Geeta Colony. So as long as it remains hidden, there is not much concern. The serious concern is that I am immobile and you have been identified. So how do we proceed? I haven't talked to any of my distributors or suppliers and worst of all Baadshaah. He must be hunting for me like a crazy. But I don't talk to any of them from inside this house. Unless I am able to move out, I do not want to get in touch with any of them."

Rahul entered the room. Rocky asked him, "Rahul, when do you think I will be able to start working again?"

"You have recovered much faster than I thought. But the problem is that the bullets had penetrated deep and so you may not be able to walk properly for a pretty long time. Further, movements may hamper healing of the wounds at least in the next three – four days. But with pain and a little limp, you should be able to walk and do all other things on your own within a week. But do not expect to be able to carry out activities requiring quick and demanding physical movements. In short, I am sorry to say, you may never be able to go back to perform the security duties."

Rocky became even more gloomy hearing this. His dream of earning a billion dollars through one small operation had so far only been getting delayed. But now it seemed to be getting beyond his reach. No doubt he now had a dependable accomplice. But she had panicked in the far smaller operation. Taking up such a job would be too much for her. Probably she should be groomed a little more with smaller less demanding jobs. Confinement to bed and availability of a partner was probably a blessing in disguise. He could think more and plan better now, for the next few days. But will his sponsors wait that long?

38

Head of the IT department stood silently with his eyes downcast and head bowed. Shiv Prasad was furious. "What kind of security arrangements we have here? If we can't have proper surveillance inside our own office, what can people expect from us? Why had the surveillance system shut down? Look into every aspect. I have a fear somebody may be conniving with the criminals and may have shut down the system."

"No, sir! I am sure the shut down was not deliberate. No one did this. There was a voltage fluctuation in the evening yesterday, which burnt out part of the system. We got that in the morning and installed it. Sir, it took just two hours to fix it. No one else can get this thing fixed in two hours."

"Two hours may be nothing for you, but it gave the criminal an easy escape, without leaving a trace. We do not have any picture of her."

He then called the police artist and asked him to get the details from Elizabeth and himself to draw a picture of Shailaja. He also asked Elizabeth to get the details of the car from the Road Transport Authorities. However, he did not expect much success from the car details.

They were once again left without a clue, ironically, after having almost nabbed the criminals. The luck also seemed to be going against them. The surveillance system in the office had been working alright, but when they needed it most, it was shut down. How can there be such a coincidence? But actually Shiv Prasad was not very right to think so. The surveillance system was often shut down for various reasons. Since it was never required in the past, no one took such shut downs so seriously. No one ever enquired about it. It was absolutely normal to bring the system in operation after a few hours shut down due to such reasons.

The phone rang. Elizabeth informed him that the Chief wanted to see him. A few minutes later he was once again narrating the whole story of Mr. India, his meeting with Anil, the killing on Akbar road, attack on himself in his office and the most recent incident at the ridge. Last time when he had told all these things, he seemed to have accepted them and had issued instructions to get red goggles for some of the security personnel involved with VVIP security. But today he appeared to be more skeptical.

He finally said in a low voice, "Shiv Prasad, somehow, these stories are not getting accepted at the top level. In fact people even disbelieve the Mr. India incidents and dismiss them off as a political or publicity stunt, because the whole thing had ended as abruptly as it had started, and then no one ever talked about these things for over two decades. Now the theory being circulated is that some anti-national elements, taking the advantage of those old stories, are trying to kill the Prime Minister. Incidentally, since you are the person who initiated this Mr. India story, suspicion surrounds you too. The CBI has been looking into your antecedents. Fortunately your reputation is very strong. Nothing has been found so far, but it does not mean that you are out in the clear. Amar Sinh Rathore too had a similar unblemished record, but he is still in the lock up. No one believes that he saw someone with red goggles who was not visible with naked eyes."

"But why the investigating agencies did not check the blood marks on the ground and out side the Parliament house? Why they do not explain the absence of all bullets from the Parliament House premises? If the gun was fired, the bullets must have hit something and must be found. If nowhere, then on the walls."

"Was there any blood mark? No one has ever stated that. Where was it? How do you know it? And if you had noticed it, why didn't you report it? Yes, I do wonder why a serious thought is not being given to the lost bullets."

"I had noticed the blood marks on the evening of the same day. I had entered the premises using my personal contacts with one of the officers here. You are aware we are not supposed to be intervening into the security affairs of the Parliament house or the VVIPs. For the goggles also I had used your influence. I tried talking to my friend about these, but he brushed me aside saying that the agency responsible for conducting enquiry were doing their job and we should not interfere."

"Yes I recall that. In fact even I was pooh-poohed when I talked about the red goggles. But then my friend agreed to provide one set to one of his officers on the VVIP duty, more like a personal favour. Now he has warned me also that if this incident takes a more serious turn, I could also get some heat from it."

"What do you suggest now?"

"We have to catch hold of this guy or at least this gadget."

"We had got hold of the gadget, and in fact I even tried it on myself. It really works. But we missed and lost it again."

"What support do you need from me?"

"Please try to convince the top brass. Get red goggles issued to at least one person in every team of security officers.

The terrorist is free, and has his gadget. I am not sure how many pieces of such gadgets they have. But I have seen a girl also using it. So there are at least two users. My guess is each has one's own set of magic band. Thus we cannot rest assured even after we get hold of one gadget or arrest one person."

Chief nodded in agreement. But he realized how difficult it was going to be.

39

Shailaja was pleasantly surprised to see the very wide smile spread across the face of Rocky. He had the morning news paper in his hand and his eyes seemed to be lost in some dreams.

"Something very interesting." She exclaimed.

"Yes, of course!" He extended the news paper towards her.

She could not figure what was making him so joyous. She looked at him questioningly. He pointed a finger to the news item about a new aircraft being inducted by Air India.

"What's so good about it?" She asked.

"Read the whole news. I guess you will understand."

She read the whole news. It was a new type of aircraft being inducted. The first plane was to be delivered next week in Delhi. The Prime Minister, some other ministers, bureaucrats and media personnel would take the first trial flight lasting about an hour. The media would be briefed about the aircraft on this flight and they could also interview the Prime Minister.

Shailaja still could not understand why should this news give so much of pleasure to Rocky. Her expression remained puzzled.

"Look! Try to find out who amongst female journalists have got an invitation to this press conference. We shall get the entry pass from her. Security arrangements at the media offices are not strong enough. In fact, there is hardly any security arrangement. You can easily get everything you want, even an identity card. Again, replicating an identity card of a journalist is a child's play! We have been replicating even passports and visas. So that should be the easy part. You will join the entourage posing as this journalist. I am sure this f***ing Shiv Prasad would have made elaborate arrangements for red flash lights to locate me – if it is not possible on the outside due to bright sun light, then inside the aircraft and at all entry points. So, my going in an invisible manner would not be possible."

"But what do you expect me to do there, without any arms? Interview the Prime minister? Definitely no journalist would be allowed to carry even a pencil sharpener as a weapon."

"Of course not!" His smile deepened. "I will manage to reach the aircraft. Not through the usual routes. I will get into any carriage entering the airport - say one carrying catering material for any domestic flight. I am sure no red light surveillance would be carried out for these vehicles. So I would enter the airport premises – the tarmac. And I will wait there for all guests to arrive. I am pretty sure that again red light surveillance would not be there at the entry to the aircraft – that is at the side from where services personnel and supplies are brought. Once inside the aircraft, I will remove the magic band – I don't think in that large crowd there will be anyone to notice addition of a stranger. You will have to help me in several things. Just don't lose your cool. Insha-Allah this time we will be successful." He copied the style of Baadshaah. He was rejoicing the thought of how the news would be broken to him. What was making him happier was the timing of this event. It was still a week away and so he would have recovered completely, ready to take up this assignment.

....

Shailaja disguised herself as a muslim woman, complete with a burqa. This gave her some reprieve from the alert eyes who might have been looking for a look-a-like of Shailaja. They were confident that her pictures must have been circulated all around and since it was such a recent event, must be fresh in the memory of some one. She took the magic band in her bag, and left home in an old Maruti Alto.

Near the newspaper office, she parked the car, came out and following the instructions of Rocky, walked in to a secluded area. The next minute she was out of that area, invisible to all naked eyes. She silently entered the newspaper office without any one trying to stop her or ask anything. Rocky was right. There was hardly any security worth the name. The door frame metal detector did exist. Also all hand bags were getting checked, but the level of seriousness, degree of alertness were low. It appeared to be just a routine checking by complacent staff.

She walked to the chamber of the Chief Editor. A bored peon sat outside the closed door. She waited for someone to either enter or exit from the room. Luckily the Chief Editor himself came out in a few minutes and began moving towards the news desk. She quickly entered the room before the door could close. She sat down on the Chief Editor's chair and began searching all letters and covers. There was no one inside and she could easily pick up any documents she wanted. She soon found what she had been looking for. The letter from the Press Information Bureau, intimating about the inaugural acceptance flight of Air India, inviting the Chief Editor or his representative. The Chief Editor had scribbled something on it. It read, "I will be away. Madhulika to please attend."

Happily Shailaja began waiting for someone to enter the room. The peon entered soon enough with some papers, kept them on the table and began walking out. Shailaja followed him and went out of the room. Now she began looking for Madhulika's cabin. Madhulika was a senior correspondent and shared her room with another senior correspondent. The door of the room was open and both the senior correspondents sat with piles of papers and a pencil in hand reading and marking them. Madhulika was a middle aged woman. Being a senior correspondent, she was probably well known also in media circles. Impersonating her would be difficult, thought Shailaja. She went close to her and stood on her side. Her bag was lying on the side table. Shailaja kept on watching her working with full concentration. Then she slowly slid the zip of her bag. She did not notice anything. Shailaja inserted her fingers into the narrow opening of the bag. She could feel the identity card, pulled it out, hurriedly went out of her room and entered the women's washroom. There was no one inside. She got into the toilet, took out the phone and clicked several pictures of both sides of the card. Satisfied, she put the mobile phone back in her bag, walked to Madhulika's office and slid the identity card back into her bag as she had taken it out. Then she came out of the news paper building, took out the magic band and got into her car. The whole operation took no more than two hours and went smooth as silk! She felt quite happy.

....

Shailaja drove the car to a deserted street near Vasant Kunj. Rocky sat on the passenger side. She parked the car and Rocky took out the phone.

"You finally got time to call?" Thundered Baadshaah from the other side.

"You must have read the news papers. I have been shot seriously and was almost on death bed. I am still carrying out my work. You should appreciate, not shout."

"Firstly, getting shot or dying is normal in our business. There is nothing unusual about it. If you are afraid of getting shot or dying, leave this business and start a travel agency. Second, the news was about a security officer shooting. Not you. Third, even this mission failed miserably. Are you worth anything?"

"Well, the security officer had been set up by me." Rocky lied, "But he goofed up. Instead of shooting the Prime Minister, he shot me, who was standing very close to the Prime minister in invisible form. Finally, I have not yet given up. I have planned the next mission. It will be executed very shortly. But I need your help."

"You only keep taking help. But you never perform." Baadshaah was still sarcastic. "Ok what help you need? Another toy, because you lost the last one too?"

"No. It is a much smaller job. An old lady has to be kidnapped and kept out of circulation for about six to eight hours."

"What? Are you joking? Now you need my help for such petty jobs? And you think I will be involved in such things? You must be out of your mind."

"I can certainly get local help." Rocky answered, "But they are not dependable. The lady is smart. A media person. If anything leaks out or my operative goofs up, this next mission will also fail. I don't want it to fail for such small reason."

"Ok. Keep the phone on at 3 pm tomorrow. Somebody will contact to get details and finalise the action plan. But if the mission fails, please remember, my men can trace you out of hell or heaven and make rest of your life worse than hell."

"Yes, I know that." Said Rocky in a grim voice.

....

Madhulika was getting late. She quickly locked the door and briskly walked out. The invitation clearly indicated that due to security reasons all guests were supposed to arrive by 7 AM and no one would be allowed after that, although the flight was to start at 9 AM. From home to airport would take not less than one hour even in this morning non-peak hour. And it was close to six already. The next problem would be getting a taxi or auto. The taxi stand was not far but the taxi drivers nagged a lot about the fare. If she was in a hurry, she would have to accept any absurd fare demand from these rogues. But she was in luck. As soon as she came on the street, a taxi was crawling by. She hailed it, and asked if he would take her to the airport. The driver did not say anything. He bent left wards, took his hand out and lowered the fare meter, signaling her to hop in. She got in, asking him to move fast and the taxi zoomed out. She relaxed, resting her head on the headrest and closing her eyes.

After about fifteen minutes she opened her eyes to see where they had reached, but could not orient herself. The route did not appear to be the regular route to the airport. She kept trying to figure her location for a while and then realized that the taxi was moving towards Greater Noida.

"Hey, where are you taking me? I have to go to the airport." She shouted.

The driver turned his head to look at her, looking perplexed. "Is it? But you said Greater Noida."

"How can that be? I have never said Greater Noida. You must be sleeping. And I have lost some precious time in this." She was really worried that with this fifteen minutes lost and the additional distance to be covered, she may not be able to reach the airport in time. The driver stopped the car, ostensibly to take a U-turn. But as the car stopped, he turned taking out a pistol and asked her to hand over her cell phone.

The street to Greater Noida is not a very busy street. Particularly at this early hour there is hardly any traffic. Looting, arson, rapes and murders are not very uncommon in this area. At her age, and less than average looks, Madhulika did not expect rape to be the motive. She kept her cool and said, "Look *bhaiya*, I have very little money, but you may keep it. You may also keep the cell phone. But I have a very important meeting to attend. Please drop me at any point from where I can get another taxi."

The man did not say a word. He took the phone, took out some adhesive tape and tied her hands and then the mouth. He began driving in the same direction. After some time he took a left turn to get into a lane and stopped in front of what looked like a deserted shop. He pulled the shutter up, pushed her inside. There were a few chairs and a table inside and nothing else. It was all very dusty indicating that no one had entered here for a long time. He made her sit on one of the dirty chairs, took out the adhesive tape again and tied her hand to the arm rest of the chair. Then he tied her legs also to the legs of the chair and without a word just walked out, pulling the shutter down again behind him.

Madhulika could not understand anything. It was impossible to imagine that the taxi driver had done all this just to get her cell phone - a cheap old model not costing more than two- three thousand rupees. He had not made any effort to snatch her money or gold ear rings or chain. No effort towards any sexual offence. She could not recall any event which could have annoyed some one to such an extent so as to kidnap her. The only possibility which made sense was that someone did not want her to attend this VVIP program. But why? In any case, he had been successful. There was no way she could reach the airport in time. There was no way she could even inform anyone of her situation. The person doing it intended no harm to her. Even the way he had tied her and left appeared amateurish. But now she had to get free quickly. No one probably ever came here and if she did not make efforts herself, she would finally starve to death. She tried to get her arms freed. But the tape was tightly wound round. She kept on moving them left and right, and saw the tape getting slightly distorted. Her arms were getting bruised and it was hurting. But the choice was between getting the bruises and starving to death in this confinement. She kept trying. If her mouth was not taped, she could have bent and used her teeth to cut and pull the tape. Her fingers were free but the mouth did not reach the fingers so there was no way she could use them to pull out the tape from her mouth. She looked around again but found nothing which could be used to free herself. After about two hours' efforts, the tape got loose enough to allow her hand to move to some extent. She bent down. Her mouth could now be reached with the fingers. She started scraping the end of the tape on her mouth with the nails. This was easier than turning the hands. In about twenty minutes, the tape could be pulled out. She took a long relaxed breath. It appeared a great achievement. Then she got down to work again. She bent and caught hold of the tape around her wrist. It could be easily cut with her teeth. In about three hours she had freed herself of the bondage. But still she was locked up in a shop. From the bottom of the shutter some light came. But the gap was not wide enough to allow her to look outside. She tried to lift the shutter but could not. She remembered it was an isolated place. No one may be around. But this was her only option. She began banging on the shutter.

40

Shailaja waited long enough for the visitors to get cleared as she did not want anyone to point out that she was not Madhulika. When the counter was free, she walked up to the security officer and presented a copy of the invitation letter and her identity card. He looked at the invitation letter and then began checking in his list of the invited guests. Finally he tick marked one name, looked at the identity card more carefully and then at her face. Her heart was beating so hard she thought he may be able to hear the sound. She looked scared. The guard could feel her unease and asked, "What is your name?"

"M.. Madhulika. Madhulika Chandra. She said in a shaky voice. Guard became a little suspicious because of her nervousness. He shot another question, "Which paper do you work for?"

"Times…. National Capital Times."

"How long have you been with this news paper?"

Shailaja had no idea. She had begun sweating. But she had to somehow manage. "Long enough. Several years." She realized that the guard was getting suspicious because of her nervousness and she must give some explanation for this nervousness to come out of his grilling. "Actually I got so late, I had to run. And I am still afraid that I might have missed it. I am not so late, isn't it?"

The guard pushed her identity card and invitation back to her and answered indifferently, "No not too late. The flight is at nine. It is still seven thirty."

She walked past the counter, through security and reached the noisy lounge where all the journalists were seated enjoying coffee, snacks and gossips. They all saw her but no one bothered to ask her anything. She took a sigh of relief and like others poured a cup of coffee for herself and sat down on a sofa, where two middle aged journalists sat discussing something in a not too loud voice. They looked at her, but continued their dialogue without disturbing her.

Some of the journalists tried to get into conversation with her, telling her that they had never seen her. She had been coached in detail by Rocky. She explained that she was from a large business house which was planning to get into aviation business. She was not supposed to talk much about this business venture at this stage as it was still being negotiated and being kept confidential. She had got a special invitation to attend this inaugural flight. They did not probe much after this, wished her and her company good luck and left her alone. She was relieved when boarding was announced. She quickly walked to almost middle of the plane, occupied an aisle seat and began watching the boarding gentry. After almost all the journalists had boarded, senior bureaucrats and some MPs came in. They were all seated in the front business class seats. The first two rows were apparently reserved for the Prime Minister and his close associates. But then she saw Shiv Prasad and Elizabeth walking in. She held her breath. Quickly took out her note book and pencil and began frantically writing something, keeping her face almost buried in the notebook. She saw from the corner of her eyes and when was confident that they had walked past her and occupied some seats in the latter half of the plane, took out her handkerchief to wipe the moisture off her forehead.

41

The services and supplies to the airlines are loaded in to large sized trucks and then driven into the airport from another entry. This side of the airport is relatively free of traffic and general hustle bustle. Here airline catering companies, courier service companies and similar services have their stores, kitchens and laundries etc. The street does not have much of passenger traffic. Only large size container trucks are found. Rocky stood in this alley looking for his best opportunity. He walked into the compound of a flight kitchen company. A truck was coming out of the building. It would soon be heading to the airport. The driver stopped the vehicle out side the building and went in with some papers. Rocky climbed into the vehicle and occupied the passenger side. In a couple of minutes, the driver came back and started the truck. He was out of the compound and reached the entry gate to the airport. The driver took out the papers to show to the security guard. He opened the passenger side door and looked in, and went back to open the rear of the truck for inspection. After the inspection, the driver came back to his seat and the guard opened the gate. In a couple of minutes they were inside the airport premises. The truck kept on moving and then stopped near a parked aircraft. The driver came out to talk to some other persons standing there. Rocky too came out. He could identify the gleaming new Air India plane from a distance. He walked to it. It was connected through an aerobridge. The aerobridge had stairs through which service personnel went up and down. Rocky thought of going up through the same but then decided against it. There was a possibility of some security men or special security measures on this side. There was considerable time before they may start boarding. Getting in so early was inviting trouble. He walked to a parked vehicle nearby and sat in looking around carefully to plan his actions in case of any problems. This plane was being given special care. Naturally. It had been connected to the aerobridge so early and service and security personnel were going in and coming out continuously. From the vehicle where Rocky had taken refuge, he was able to watch the movements through the narrow window on the side of the aerobridge also. The activities were getting more and more frenzied. A truck had parked on the starboard side of the plane, apparently to load catering material. This was the moment Rocky had been waiting for. He quickly reached the truck and boarded the platform which would soon be docking with the plane. He silently stood in a corner waiting for it to be lifted. The operator also came on the platform and began raising it. It reached the level of the plane and was docked. The operator peeped inside the small opening on the gate of the plane and signaled to the airhostess. After the signals were exchanged, the gate of the plane opened. The operator moved back to open the door of the container. Rocky coolly walked inside the plane. The security personnel were carrying out a last minute check of all bins and seat pockets. He kept on standing in the corner without coming in any one's way. The security personnel left the plane in a few minutes and Rocky walked down the aisle towards the last row. He took a seat and began waiting for the guests to arrive. At around eight thirty they started boarding. He was relieved to see Shailaja also boarding. She appeared to be calm and composed. She occupied an aisle seat in the middle of the plane. His scheme had been working perfectly. He felt his AK47 and felt the adrenalin rising in himself. And then the flow of adrenalin shot up. He saw Shiv Prasad and Elizabeth also entering the plane. This was a bad omen, he thought. He noticed Shailaja quickly burying herself in her note book. Shiv Prasad was intently watching every face. Many of them seemed to be knowing him. They waved to him and he too responded by waving to them. About three seats before Shailaja's, he stopped and was looking intently at her. She was busy writing something in her notebook without lifting her face. Shiv Prasad kept looking at her while passing her, but did not stop or say anything. He reached almost the back end of the plane leaving just about five to six rows and then occupied the aisle seat, asking Elizabeth to occupy the aisle seat of the opposite side. Rocky heaved a sigh of relief.

42

Shiv Prasad and Elizabeth had reached the airport at seven AM. Shiv Prasad had worked very hard to convince the Chief to get some red lights installed at the security hold area and the entry to the aircraft. He had also got a couple of security officers red goggles with instructions to keep using them every four to five minutes, to locate things which were not visible without those glasses. Shiv Prasad was confident that Aidni Rm would not miss this opportunity to strike. A large part of the Cabinet, several top level bureaucrats, chiefs of some of the PSUs and a large number of media personnel were going to be on board. For a terrorist, the only better opportunity could be the Republic Day Parade. This guy had missed out on that. He will not spare any effort to use this moment. He was himself silently supervising all activities along with the regular security officers. The regular security officers had not quite appreciated interference of an 'outsider', but the orders were to co-operate with him. His full attention was grabbed by the red light wielding guards. But he had not been able to see any untoward movements.

Shiv Prasad was still not feeling assured after everyone had checked in. His instinct said something had been escaping his and everyone else's attention. But they had noticed nothing abnormal. He entered the aircraft after all journalists and bureaucrats had entered and only the VVIPs had to enter. He was looking intently at all the faces to find any suspicious persons. He noticed one of the lady journalists writing furiously in her note book. He kept watching her for some time. But she did not look up. She was some young new journalist probably eager to make some impression on her boss. He walked towards the back of the plane. It was a huge plane and the last few seats were going to remain vacant. From the back of the plane he could have a good direct view of all activities and even start taking timely actions. But the red lights at the security area had been working alright and the security personnel were alert and had been watching carefully all movements in the red light area. He was beginning to think that Aidni Rm had finally decided to miss this opportunity.

The VVIPs arrived almost on the dot. The doors of the plane were shut and announcements began. Soon the plane was being towed back.

43

The plane had attained a level height. Seat belt sign was switched off and a technical person from the Airline got up, walked up to the front of the plane and announced that they would now start the presentation on the capabilities and special features of this plane while they could enjoy the hospitality of the airline.

A loud voice suddenly took over everyone by surprise, It was not from the public address system. It was not the soft voice of the technical person. It was not from the cockpit. It came from the backside of the plane. "Dear Mr. Prime Minister, and all our guests! You are all advised not to look behind, not to try to get up from your seats. Raise your hands above your heads and keep sitting without any movements."

One of the SPG officers sitting right behind the Prime Minister sprang, in one stroke switched off the lights of the plane. But there was a lot of light coming from the windows. Two officers lied down on the ground and with astonishing speed began crawling in the aisle towards the rear. Some gunshots were heard and the two became still where they were. Blood began spilling out of their head and backs. Smell of gunfire spread in the cabin. Stunned silence followed for a few moments. The voice came again. "Thank you, SPG officers, for giving me the opportunity for an excellent demonstration! I hope others will take a lesson! But if there are some more brave hearts, they may like to test me again!"

The atmosphere became very tense. Everyone was thinking of how to wriggle out of the situation or do something brave. But the only ones who could be expected to do something were the SPG officials. Two of them had already given their lives. Presently they all were like sitting ducks for the terrorist who had not only broken into the highest security ring, but had also killed a couple of commandoes and continued to enjoy a commanding position. There were so many media personnel with cameramen. This could be the most exciting piece of news shooting the TRPs to unimaginable heights…. Provided they survived!

There was a pause. The voice came again, "I don't see hands rising above heads. Why do you want me to waste my bullets on you?" There was a laugh, and then the voice sounded even more gruff, "All of you are in the range of my gun. And I can crash this plane in one second. Any smart move would mean killing this entire gentry immediately. If you want another demo, please try! But do not test my patience. I don't have enough of it."

Every one in the plane raised hands above heads. The few more commandoes occupying the seats behind the Prime Minister felt helpless. They could not do anything until the attacker came forward. Now they all were sitting with their backs to the terrorist and were not in a position to think or plan anything. The two who had tried, had already lost their lives, achieving nothing but a futile martyrdom. Their bodies lay in the middle of aisle. Blood was oozing out and spreading over the carpet. Shiv Prasad's worst fears had come true. The sound came again, "Mr. Shiv Prasad, I don't see your hands. Death for a simple reason of not raising hands would sound too stupid. Why don't you come out and do something brave like these two clowns?"

So he knew exactly where he was sitting. Shiv Prasad was more scared that if one of the bullets punches a hole in a window pane, the cabin pressure would be lost. The plane was flying at not less than thirty thousand feet. Loss of pressure at this altitude meant immediate death of everyone in the plane. The sound was coming from behind him. He regretted not having taken the last row. Now there was no way he could turn his head and see who was it and where he sat. He had his red goggles in his pocket, he could take it out but how to look back? He figured, the terrorist will be able to see his raised hands but what he did in the few seconds before raising the hand, would not be known. He took out the goggles and put on his eyes while raising the hands.

The sound came again, "Thank you, Shiv Prasad! You are not as stupid as I thought! Well, dear SPG officers, now it is time that you too sat comfortably without the unnecessary load of those fire arms. My colleague will help you! She will collect these from you. Please do not make any efforts to fool her or to overpower her. We are a suicide team and won't think twice before shooting ourselves also. This would mean instant death to all of you."

Shiv Prasad saw Shailaja getting up from her seat and moving forward towards the Prime Minister's seat. On the aisle the blood from the dead bodies of the two martyrs was spread over a considerable area. She did not make any effort to avoid it. She just walked over it and on their bodies with contempt. Every one in the plane got overwhelmed with nausea and hatred for her. Shiv Prasad once again repented at not having checked her in spite of the doubt that had crept in to his mind while boarding the plane.

She reached the front part and began collecting all the guns from the SPG officers. Shiv Prasad was filled with shame and agony to watch such highly trained officers meekly handing over their guns to her. She looked a professional criminal unlike what she looked like when he had seen her last time. He was surprised how she could change so fast. She was insisting that they take out their revolvers and other smaller firearms also to her. She took them and dumped in the toilet in the front side of the aircraft. Finally she held one AK47 in her hand and stood in front of the Prime Minister, pointing it at him. Shiv Prasad was trying to get any sounds of movement from the back of the plane but due to the noise of the plane, nothing could be heard. And then he saw through his red goggles Aidni Rm with another AK47 walking with a limp towards the front. As he passed Shiv Prasad, he looked sideways at him with a crooked smile. Shiv Prasad kept on sitting as if was not seeing anything, but as soon as Aidni Rm passed his seat, he did not lose any time. With the swiftness of a cheetah, he grabbed him, covered his mouth with his palm before he could scream and pulled him into his row, himself moving towards the window side. Aidni Rm could not scream, could not even defend himself. He was over confident and had not expected any such attack on himself. But his strength itself turned out to be his biggest mistake. He was confident that if any one attacks him, Shailaja would shoot the Prime Minister. So no one would have the courage to meddle with him. He had been invisible. What he had failed to visualize was that he was also invisible to his accomplice, Shailaja. When Shiv Prasad so swiftly captured him she did not even come to know. She was concentrating on the front row and the SPG officials, who could pose a real threat to her. She knew that Aidni Rm would be now walking up to her to take control of the situation.

Elizabeth saw the strange movements of Shiv Prasad. She was the only one in the plane who could guess what might have happened. She opened her bag and quickly threw some nylon cords and adhesive tapes towards Shiv Prasad. He plastered his mouth with the tape and moved on to tie him up with the cords. Then he slipped the magic band out of his wrist, put it on his own wrist. He took the AK47 which was with Aidni RM and handed over to Elizabeth. Then he coolly walked up the aisle towards Shailaja. He reached her, patted her on the shoulder and took the gun from her. As soon as the gun was in his hand, he kicked her to make her fall on the ground, stepped on her neck and shouted, "Dear friends, the terrorists have been captured. The Prime Minister and all of you are safe, I request not to panic. The security officers may please collect their guns now."

But no one moved. He had not realized that the people were not able to see him. The disappearance of AK47 from Shailaja's hand, her sudden fall and lying on ground in such a precarious condition could not be understood by any one. He pulled the magic band out of his wrist and became visible. Now the people could see what had actually happened. The security personnel rushed to take control of their guns. Shiv Prasad handed over the gun in his hand to one of the officers, pulled Shailaja up and dragged her to the rear of the plane. Aidni Rm lied there on the seat moaning and trying to free himself. Shiv Prasad signaled Elizabeth to pass on some more cords. They tied Shailaja also.

EPILOGUE

When Elizabeth entered his office, Shiv Prasad sat in his usual "deep thinking" posture with both elbows on the table and palms covering eyes and forehead. The coffee after having spread its aroma in the room, was lying cold and neglected in the mug. She looked a little puzzled. She was under impression that the most complicated case had been solved, all news papers and TV channels had been singing praises of Shiv Prasad. Even the Prime Minister had personally congratulated Shiv Prasad. The festivities were not even over and some new problem had taken over her boss. In fact she had come today with one of her own problems. While she was overjoyed with the success of Shiv Prasad and overwhelmed with his bravery, intelligence, nationalism and dutifulness, the deep lying sting in her had become more accentuated. She had tears of joy out of their success and tears of sorrow for the untold, unexplained pain she had been experiencing for so many days. She intended to convey him her decision of resigning from the force. But he seemed to have fallen into another new problem. She did not have the heart to break any unpleasant news to him in such a situation. She sat down as usual, playing with her pencil, drawing absurd lines on her pad, waiting for him to break the silence.

Finally he lifted his head to look at her. She could not read his mind. Whether he was still thinking or he wanted to say something or the matter was highly confidential and could not be shared. She kept looking at his face still waiting for him to speak.

"Liz, I want to tell you something." Shiv Prasad said in a low voice. She did not say anything, just kept looking at him to hear whatever he had to say. But her own proposition was almost bursting to come out of her mouth. She may not be able to assist him in any further assignments because she was planning to quit. Why? She couldn't tell. She had been suffering too much. Why? Again she couldn't tell. What was she suffering? How could she tell? But it had been enough. She had no alternative but to quit. Probably for no reasons. The thought of quitting was bringing tears to her eyes. It was difficult to keep herself under control. But whatever happens, she must quit now. Shiv Prasad was also probably trying to read her mind.

His lips quivered. Words were trying to come out. His voice became lower. He touched her hand and almost whispered, "Liz, I love you."

Elizabeth could not believe her ears. She never thought Shiv Prasad was even aware of the existence of these three words. She thought he was completely devoid of such delicate feelings. And she stood completely mistaken. He was, after all as humane as she herself was. Tears of joy filled her eyes. The whole world seemed to be revolving round her. She lost sense of her existence. She was flying up in the endless sky. Cold crisp breeze surrounding her, kissing her passionately. Thousands of church bells were ringing around her and between the chimes of the bells, slow whispering voice of Shiv Prasad was echoing, 'I do…I do.. I do'.

END

ABOUT THE AUTHOR

Ashok Varma is an engineer by qualification and has been working with Oil and Natural Gas Corporation Ltd, the national oil company of India, since 1978. His work made him to travel not only across the length and breadth of the country but also to several countries of the world and that too to very remote parts of these countries such as Sakhalin islands, Siberia, Caspian Sea, North Sea, Trinidad, Hokkaido, Bogota etc. Edny Arem is his first attempt at writing a novel.